Ellora's Cave Publishing, Inc.
PO Box 787
Hudson, OH 44236-0787

ISBN: 1-84360-402-7

Edited by Sheri Ross Carucci
Cover art by Darrell King

Warning: The following material contains strong sexual content
meant for mature readers. *Slave Planet* has been rated NC17,
erotic. We strongly suggest storing this book in a place where
young readers not meant to view it are unlikely to happen upon
it. That said, enjoy…

SLAVE PLANET

Written by

J.W. McKenna

Also by J.W. McKenna:

Slave Planet (bondage/sci-fi)

The Hunted (anthology)

Darkest Hour (bondage)

Ellora's Cave Publishing

www.ellorascave.com

Chapter 1

Pure oxygen, mixed with stimulants, hissed into the cocoon surrounding Capt. Kathryn Dyson. The dark-haired woman didn't move at first, "sleeping the sleep of the dead," as space boomers called it. Finally, her eyes fluttered. She stirred, her t-shirt shifting over her breasts. She opened her eyes and looked around, confused, groggy.

Awareness returned slowly. Her eyes opened wide, then narrowed as she focused on the panel near her right hand. Green. *Good,* she thought. *It's not an emergency.* The cocoon was designed to wake her if something had gone wrong during the long flight. A green board told her that she had been awakened on time.

Kate hit the switch, venting the oxygen and allowing it to be replaced by ordinary air. Another switch caused the cocoon's lid to hiss open. She spent a few minutes getting her bearings, then struggled with her straps to free herself. As she sat up, she smiled wryly at the paper panties that remained bunched by her left hand. Cryosleep required many long months motionless while the ship hurled through empty space. NASA, in its wisdom, decided that cloth panties might cause yeast infections during the long slumber. Paper panties that breathed were the official sleepwear, which most women grudgingly accepted.

Kate, however, didn't buy it. Rather than wear the damn things, she preferred to "go bare." Since she was captain, she would be the last to sleep and the first to awaken. It was her right to wear what she wanted — or to wear nothing at all.

She tossed the panties into the trash recycler and paused to look over her sleeping crew. The four remaining cocoons were reading green. Good. She didn't really trust these damn things any more than she trusted a soda machine to give her correct change. She walked the line, checking the faces of each of her crew. All were women, dressed in tee-shirts and those silly panties, their long legs partially obscured by the darkened cocoons. They would be awakened soon. In the meantime, there was time to check out the ship and their journey.

Kate half-floated, half-padded barefoot to her quarters, cognizant of the low gravity. On long trips like this, the gravity field was kept weak until they approached their destination. There was no need to waste energy. Now, just days away from the unexplored system, the gravity field would strengthen until their "land legs" returned in time for exploration — if the opportunity presented itself. A big if.

She took a quick shower. A space shower was quite the experience for those not familiar with the procedure. Water was a premium on board, so showers consisted of a blast of droplets to wet the body, followed by a scrubbing down with a special soap, then another blast to rinse. A fan sucked the mixture away. Kate never quite got used to it and she had been an astronaut for twelve years.

Walking naked from the shower, she relished these few minutes alone. A long space voyage was an exercise in forced civility with one's crewmates. NASA selected the crew, and Kate didn't find their personalities fit in all cases — but they were all professionals and would make this trip successful. They had to.

Kate paused, standing there in the nude, thinking about Brian and the last time they made love, so many months ago. Her nipples hardened in the processed air. Kate unselfconsciously touched her breasts, pretending it was Brian's hands stroking her. Her mind easily recalled the evening, as it was just a few nights ago as far as she was concerned. Cryosleep has a way of compacting time.

She smiled and let her fingers drift down to brush her smooth mound below her navel. She felt a little naughty. Here she was, captain of NASA's most expensive ship built to date and she was seriously thinking of…well, no, she wouldn't. Would she?

She should get dressed, she told herself. Many things to do. Her mind betrayed her, bringing up the image of Brian next to her in bed, his hard muscles a contrast to her soft curves. He was hard somewhere else as well, she remembered. Brian had been deliciously unabashed, encouraging her gaze upon him. If anything, it made him harder. His cock was a very nice shape — thick and veiny with a bulbous head that could make her salivate.

Kate remembered leaning down to kiss it, knowing that these sights, these actions, would have to last her for nearly two years — longer for him. His smell enveloped her, a musky, sexy, piquant scent that caused the lips of her wet slit to part in anticipation. As her mind wandered back to that day, so did her fingers now, down past her bare mons, letting them dance along her sensitive cleft. She could feel herself getting wet. Kate eased down onto the closed toilet seat.

Brian had thrown his head back as she took him into her mouth that night and now Kate threw her own head back against the bulkhead and closed her eyes as her fingers traced a gentle track along her moist cleft. Already her clit poked out of its tender prison. She had sucked Brian's sweet cock, enjoying the sensation, the musky smell of him, until he whimpered and touched her head. "Wait," he had breathed, "I want to be in you."

Kate had laid back on their bed, relishing the way Brian had crawled over her like some sort of beast, his hardness swinging like a club underneath him. She spread her legs for him, welcoming him. She had been so wet, her cunt gaped. Her fingers, remembering, opened her cleft now and rubbed the little pearl inside.

OK, she told herself, maybe starship captains *do* masturbate after cryosleep.

Brian had placed the tip of his cock at her hot core, then paused, looking down on her. "When you're in space," he said softly, "remember this moment." Then he pressed himself into her, slowly, making her feel every inch. He slid in smoothly, so familiar, so much a part of her. This time it did not feel like the lovemaking of "old married folks," sixteen years into their relationship. They were literally star-crossed lovers who would soon be torn asunder. The orgasm that had rocked her was made sweeter and sadder because it would be the last one they would share for a long time. Of course, it wasn't. They had made love twice more during the night, like teenagers discovering sex for the first time.

Kate let the pad of her finger stroke the wet clit, dipping in for the slippery fluid. She remembered Brian taking her in front, from behind and again on their sides. She concentrated on the image of his cock thrusting into her again and again as she rubbed herself, faster and faster. In minutes, it gave her the climax she so desperately needed. "Oh god!" she shouted in the tiny bathroom. "Oh my god!"

She sagged back against the bulkhead. *I wonder if this makes me a member of the million-mile club?* She laughed at herself. "Oh, Captain Dyson, you wicked, wicked woman." Her voice sounded hollow in the silent ship. She was glad no one could hear. "OK, back to work."

As she shrugged on her pink bikini panties—non-regulation, of course—and the blue NASA coveralls, she reflected on how much this trip meant to her and to Earth. The *U.S.S. Letanya* carried the first all-female crew sent out to further the exploration of the Andromeda galaxy. Since 2053—the year faster-than-light drive had been invented—men had had the privilege of jetting around space, getting the glory, while women were reduced to mere back-up roles. In the twenty-two years since that first flight, only eleven women had been included on trips. It was time to let a woman captain an exploration, America demanded.

But why stop there? Lobbying by women's organizations and Congress finally convinced NASA that an all-female crew could be a public relations boon. It was decided the latest warp-drive ship, the *Letanya*, would be manned—er, womanned?—by an all-female crew. Capt. Kathyrn Dyson, the eldest and most experienced at 38, would lead the mission, along with four of the top female astronauts and scientists NASA had to offer.

Kate was very proud to have been chosen for such an honor, yet she still burned over the memory of her briefing at NASA headquarters in Houston. She had been called to the office of Admiral James Hunter, the decorated and beloved godfather of warp-drive exploration. It was Hunter who had gone out with Jerry Roth on the first mission to explore Andromeda, the closest galaxy at 2.2 million light years away. Without warp drive and cryosleep, such a trip would not have been possible.

After six months in stasis, Hunter and Roth awoke to a wonder never before seen by human eyes except through distant telescopes—new planetary systems, and with them, new opportunities to find life. Andromeda is a huge galaxy, one-and-a-half times as large as our own Milky Way. It stretches one-hundred-fifty thousand light years across. The astronauts had just two months to explore a handful of the thousands of suns that whirled around in the galaxy. The starship could not land on the planets they came across and the crew had no shuttle craft, so all their explorations were done with probes sent to the surfaces below.

New minerals, bacteria and plant species were discovered on one of the planets. On another world, they found some reptiles and amphibians. That they found no intelligent life didn't matter to NASA. After charting a tiny fraction of the system and exhausting their probes, Hunter and Roth returned to Earth as conquering heroes.

While they had been gone a little over a year—twelve months traveling and two months exploring—Earth had aged two years. It was Einstein's theory proven fact. This just made their safe return all the more remarkable. Ticker tape parades greeted them. Roth later left NASA to head a multinational corporation, and Hunter rose to head the agency.

His past glory didn't excuse his treatment of Kate Dyson when she was brought in to accept the assignment. Hunter told her he had been under pressure to approve the "all-girl" mission, as he kept calling it. He thought it was a bad idea.

"I'll tell you right now, I'm against this. What if you girls get stuck out there? Are you going to expect us to come rescue you because you're women?" he asked her as she stood in front of his desk, trapped between conflicting emotions. She was thrilled to be given the job, yet despised this Neanderthal who thought women needed rescuing.

"I wouldn't expect treatment any different than you give to the male astronauts," she had said, keeping her voice neutral.

"Damn right," Hunter said. "But think how that will play out at home. You get your tits in a wringer out there and we don't do anything, we'll look like uncaring jerks. This mission could be a disaster that sets NASA back 20 years."

Kate's face burned, but she said nothing for a moment. She had to be careful. She was willing to endure this abuse if it meant getting the assignment. "We won't let you down," she said lamely.

He stared at her. He knew he was being bullshitted. "I'm going to announce this all-girl mission tomorrow. I've got no choice. My Congressman made that very clear. The crew's already been selected." He handed her a folder. "But I'm telling you right now it's imperative that you don't fuck up out there. The space program depends on it."

"We'll be careful, sir."

Hunter pointed a stubby finger at her. "Off the record, I'll tell you this: If you get hung up out there, don't call us up and cry for help. That will just make things worse. It'll be better for the space program if you do an Amelia Earhart out there. If we hear from you, it'll be like the *Rochester* all over again."

Kate cringed inwardly. The *U.S.S. Rochester* was NASA's biggest failure since the *Challenger* explosion in the 1980s. Manned by four men and a token woman, the

Rochester rocketed off into the Milky Way galaxy eight years ago for a mapping mission and ran into some kind of trouble. The only radio message Earth received said they had "hit some space debris" and were attempting to make repairs.

There was a hue and cry to go rescue them until scientists pointed out that because of the lag time and the space-time continuum, it would be another six months before a ship could reach them. By that time, either they would be long dead, or they would have already returned to Earth, provided they were able to make repairs. The rescue mission would have squandered already tight resources. That didn't make anyone feel any better, but because the captain and most of the crew were men, America decided they could fend for themselves.

Unfortunately, they were never heard from again. Their fate remains a mystery to this day. Every anniversary of the launch, the media reminds the public of this failure and headlines ask the annual question: "What Happened to the *Rochester*?" A parade of "experts" would speculate on how they met their grisly end. Everyone at NASA was sick of it and most had known the *Rochester* crew personally. It just didn't do any good to keep dwelling on it.

Kate knew what was at stake when "girls" were allowed to take the newest starship in the fleet out for a quick spin. If they succeeded, they might be able to shut up assholes like Hunter. If they failed, they'd prove the bastards right.

This mission would be exceptionally crucial because it represented just the third time that a crew would attempt to land on any "Class M" planet it discovered. Advances in technology had made this feat more practical. After all, why travel two million light years or more and not visit a planet? Probes could only do so much.

In the two previous landings on planets in Andromeda's many solar systems, astronauts brought back a treasure trove of information. To date, however, none had discovered intelligent life. That remained the Holy Grail that each new crew hoped to find. Kate wanted to be the first. That would really prove the mettle of her "all-girl" crew.

The trip had an inauspicious beginning. Once the announcement was made, it didn't take long for wags to dub the new ship the *"Lesbanya."* Ha ha. Kate didn't recall the first small star ship, the *U.S.S. Dickson*, after the popular, pro-NASA president, being called some rude name just because four men led it. Following the *"Lesbanya"* crack came the jokes about PMS, women drivers and the number of suitcases they'll need on the two-year trip.

Kate felt the weight of not only the world on her shoulders, but also that of women's rights. One hundred fifty years after women got the vote in this country, and they're still considered "too delicate" for certain jobs. Kate was determined to prove them wrong.

She glided to the cockpit and strapped herself into the chair. Checking the controls, she found they were on course, on time. Coming out of warp in five hours, just ten thousand kilometers outside the section of the Andromeda system they were to explore. She ran through the diagnostics, checking every control, system and section. It took her ninety minutes before she could breathe a sigh of relief. Remarkably, the ship was shipshape. Kate smiled.

"Maybe we 'girls' can handle this after all," she murmured aloud. Of course, so far, the ship had done all the work.

The control panel beeped. The other crew members were being awakened. Kate wanted to be there.

Chapter 2

Kate stood by the cocoon as the air hissed into it, releasing her second-in- command, Commander Allyson Egerton. Of all the women in the space program, Kate was glad NASA had assigned the smart, funny, self-deprecating redhead to the crew. She had met Ally eight years ago and the two hit it off right away. Kate couldn't have picked a better, more qualified "No. 1."

She waited until Ally's eyes fluttered open, then grinned at the groggy crew woman. "Reveille was," Kate made a show of looking at her watch, "214 days ago, commander. You planning on sleeping through the entire trip?"

"Sorry, captain. Forgot to set my alarm," Ally smiled back and allowed Kate to help her from the cocoon. She pulled at her panties and grimaced. "God. Can't wait to get out of these."

Kate smiled. Ally took one look and said, "Oh, tell me you didn't, captain."

Kate laughed and wagged her finger. She had told Ally many times of her distaste for the paper panties. "Careful, that could be construed as insubordination, No. 1. However, I will tell you that being the captain gives one certain small prerogatives, including the right not to wear the god-awful things."

Ally laughed. "You'd change your tune if something had gone wrong and you were awakened half-naked twenty years in the future by horny scavengers."

Kate smiled enigmatically. "After twenty years in space, they'd better watch out for me." She wondered what Ally would have thought about her little "self-help" session a while ago.

Ally turned serious. "How we doing, sir? Board green?"

Kate nodded. Though some female commanders preferred to be called "ma'am," Kate hated the term— "sounds like a whorehouse madam or a librarian," she'd say. Over the years, "sir" had become more gender neutral, and Kate's crew learned early to call her by that respectful title. "Everything is perfect. We're about two hours from the end of warp, coming in on course, on time."

The commander breathed a sigh of relief. While Kate had told none of the other women on board about Hunter's conversation, she did share it with Ally, so they'd be on the same page if anything went wrong. Both women knew they were really on their own out here.

"Well, I've got about twenty minutes before the other capsules open, so with your permission, captain, I'd like to take a quick shower and get more presentable." The capsules were timed that way so the superior officers could be in uniform before the others woke up. It bolstered the chain of command.

Kate nodded. "Have everyone join us on the bridge when they're all freshened up." She turned away and headed back up the corridor.

One hour and fifteen minutes later, the crew had gathered on the bridge. They chatted with each other like old friends, though they had been together just four months before liftoff. Seven months in cyrosleep can make a person downright chatty, Kate supposed.

She looked them over, as if seeing them for the first time. Because the crew was so small, everyone pulled double duty except Kate. Allyson, in addition to serving as second-in-command, used her knowledge of computers to ride herd on the electronic systems.

Greta Hanson, a cool, tall blonde, served as the mission commander and the geologist. She hoped mightily that they would find a Class M planet that she could explore. As mission commander, she would lead the away team.

She was a good two inches taller than Kate and she used her physical presence to her full advantage. She was competent, but opinionated. Greta had a response to nearly every command. Kate was already tired of her. However, Greta had the credentials—a hot-shot pilot who had served three trips on previous missions.

Beth Reyes, the medical officer and anthropologist, was a tremendous asset to the mission, Kate thought. She had been a surgeon before joining NASA to satisfy her urge to visit the stars. Beth was far more than just another EMT on board. Kate didn't think there was anything she couldn't handle. A short, heavyset Latina, she had long dark hair that she normally kept up in a bun. Today, however, she wore it down after her long slumber and the brief shower to let it air dry.

Kate liked the woman—she had a good sense of humor and was eager to help the team. Kate knew if she ever got to pick her crew, Beth would be her second choice, right after Allyson.

The final member of the crew was Lt. Commander Jorja Smith, the engineer and botanist. It was her job to keep the ship running smoothly—or "hot, straight and normal," as she liked to say. At six-feet and a muscular 180 pounds, Jorja was taller than Greta and outweighed the slender Swede. Jorja called herself "big boned" and she lived life with the same appetite she had for a good meal. With the freeze-dried food out here in space, she claimed she might waste away and became a runway model when she got back.

Kate liked the woman because she wasn't flashy about her competence like Greta was. And the engineer never tried to intimidate the captain with her size. She completely trusted Jorja to fix any problem with the ship—Kate just didn't want any problems on this mission.

Kate called the chit-chat to a halt. "OK, listen up. We're about to drop out of warp and into history. You all know the importance of this mission. I want nothing to go wrong. We're going to take this one step at a time. Please double-check everything as you go.

"I know you all would love to be the first to find intelligent life. So would I. It would really put us on equal footing with the other astronauts." Everyone knew Kate meant "men."

"But it's more important to me that we do our jobs and return home safely than find anything at all. That being said, I'll be keeping our fingers crossed, the same as you." Kate looked at the chronograph. "We've got thirty-five minutes until the end of warp. We want to be strapped in and have every system checked out. You know we might run into a debris field as soon as we arrive, so I want to make sure the shields are at maximum."

"The power from the warp engines should switch over automatically," Greta put in.

Kate tried not to show her annoyance. "Yes, I know. I want Jorja to monitor that process closely." She wanted to add, "because it's her job, not yours," but she knew Greta was just being Greta.

"There are seven planets in the Denoba system, as you know. The sun is similar to ours, so we might get lucky. We should drop out of warp about ten thousand kilometers from Altair, the outermost planet. We're going to probe the first two, as we already know these gas giants can't support life as we know it. And the two planets closest to the sun are likely too hot. When we approach the fifth, fourth and third planets, in order, we'll take more time. Keep your fingers crossed."

The captain glanced over her display panel. "As you know, NASA regs require everyone to have a quick checkup after a prolonged warp sleep, so as soon as we finish our reports, I'll want Dr. Reyes to begin calling us one-by-one into sick bay."

"Will there be time for personal messages home?" Beth asked.

Kate nodded. "I know you're missing your families. After I give the report, you can tell your families how much fun you're having up here." There was nervous laughter.

Because they were so far away, communication was difficult. It took messages one hour and forty-two minutes to reach Earth and a similar amount of time for a message to return. That meant it would be at least three-and-a-half hours before NASA could respond and far longer for any personal messages to arrive from the families.

Being that far from home sobered the crew. They were completely alone out here.

Chapter 3

The *Letanya* dropped out of warp on time, only zero-point-four degrees off course. They were far enough out so they didn't risk running into anything and Kate quickly corrected the heading.

The sight before them was breathtaking. The gaseous planet, Altair, glowed green and gold in the viewport. To the left, and twenty five thousand kilometers farther away was Baran, its rings spreading out three thousand kilometers. The Denoba sun, still 130 million miles away, shone so brightly Kate had to deploy filters.

"Golly, will you look at that," Ally breathed.

"Ladies, how does it feel to be the first humans to see this sight?" Kate asked. The crew just stared in awe. A long minute passed. "All right, let's man our stations. I'm going to check in with NASA. I'll bet they're getting anxious right about now."

Kate dialed up the radio-telescope transmitter, making sure the dish was pointed precisely at Earth. One tenth of a degree of error and the message could miss the planet entirely. She swung the overhead camera until it could see the viewport over her shoulder and took a deep breath.

"*Letanya* calling Houston, *Letanya* calling Houston," she began. The intro was a mere formality—a holdover from the days when you could expect immediate response. "This is Captain Kathryn Dyson of the *Starship Letanya*. We have dropped out of warp, on time and on location in the Denoba system. All boards are green. I repeat, all boards are green. You should be receiving our initial telemetry …now." She pressed a few buttons on her console. Position, ship status and other key data are routinely sent on a sub-carrier wave along with the audio/video.

"In a few minutes, we will begin our explorations. Right now, we are looking at the two outermost planets, Altair and Baran, of the seven-planet solar system. We will be sending you data as we go, of course. We expect to explore this system and two more, as planned.

"On a personal note, I'd like to tell my family that I'm doing fine after our long sleep and miss them a great deal. Brian and Donnie, I know you've been waiting a long time to hear from me," she glanced at the chronometers along the top of the panel, "approximately one year and two months. To us, of course, it's been seven months, although it feels like merely a long winter's nap." The crew laughed nervously behind around her. It was strange, realizing that everyone on Earth was aging so rapidly compared to them. "I can't wait to hear from you and I look forward to coming home safely to you in about a year or so.

"Now, I'd like to turn the camera on Commander Allyson Egerton, so she may say a few words to her family." Kate switched the camera to the one over Ally's chair. Her No. 1 began talking to her family. She listened, quietly as each of her crew in turn told their loved ones how much they missed them.

It was such a tremendous sacrifice to come out here as explorers. Until warp speed could be increased dramatically, these long trips were an unfortunate necessity. Kate imagined it was probably the same for explorers of the New World in the 1700s, sailing off into the vast ocean in search of riches, not to return for years.

By the time the crew each had a chance before the camera, more than thirty minutes had passed. Kate told NASA they would be looking forward to hearing from them in another two hours or so and signed off.

"OK, ladies. Let's pull up our panty hose and get to work."

The *Letanya* moved past Altair at a safe distance, to make sure the heavy gravitational field didn't grab the small scout ship. The ship would be doing simple "fly-bys" of these first two planets, letting the probes do the work. Firing two probes, they recorded temperature readings, gas emissions, gravity strength, mineral deposits and bacterial activity. The readings were saved for the next broadcast home.

Three hours later, another two probes were launched at the ringed planet. The rings, like those around Saturn, were made up of ice and dirt. Two probes, fired a few minutes apart, were used because the chance of failure was certain. It was just a question of when the atmosphere would crush them. With two probes, there was a good chance that some meaningful data would be recorded in the final few seconds of their short lives.

While both these first two planets were stunning and rich in new discoveries, the crew couldn't help but let their minds wander ahead to the inner ring of planets. The Jackson Symthe Space Telescope, named after the inventor of the warp drive, had indicated that the third and fourth planets had potential to be Class M, meaning there might be a breathable atmosphere. Temperature and gravity were unknowns. Everyone was on edge, hoping they would be the first to discover a new civilization.

As they cleared the planet and headed toward Jenir, the fifth planet, the communications chime rang loudly in the cockpit. NASA was calling.

"*Letanya*, this is Houston. *Letanya*, this is Houston," the message began. Everyone dropped what she was doing as Kate put the video on the main viewer. The worn face of James Hunter filled the screen. That the man himself would show up for their first broadcast showed the crew the weight NASA was putting on their mission.

"Good day, captain and crew. We were very happy to hear the ship performed as designed and that you are safely in the Denoba system. Your initial readings are amazing even the most jaded scientists here. We can't express how proud we are of your accomplishments to date.

"I realize you have a lot of work to do, so I won't hold you up. I want to turn you over to Mission Control Commander John Phillips to give you the latest news and mission parameters. After that, we have some personal messages for all of you," Hunter said.

The crew was happy to hear they had gotten their families together so quickly. Kate knew NASA had collected videotaped greetings over the last few months in preparation of this day. There was nothing like a message from loved ones to boost morale.

The round face of Phillips appeared. He was wearing the traditional vest of the mission commander, emblazoned with their logo. The women could still see where they had each signed it so many months ago, just before they were buttoned up for the long ride.

"Hello, ladies!" His voice cheered them immediately. Phillips was the perfect choice for this mission—brilliant, funny, and inventive. If anything went wrong, they all believed Phillips would be able to get them back home — and make them laugh about it along the way. Phillips held up a piece of paper. "Now, boomers, before we get started, it appears none of you filed your income tax returns this past April. The IRS has informed me that, upon return, you collectively owe," he pretended to read from the sheet, "two hundred fifty-seven thousand, four hundred twenty-nine dollars and 89 cents. Unless you can pay upon landing, your ship will be confiscated for back taxes."

Kate and the others laughed at the lame joke. It was typical of Phillips to try to relax the tension. "OK," he tossed the paper over his shoulder. "Let's get down to business, shall we?" He went on with the changes in the mission, none major, and updated the crew on some world events.

Finally, he got to the part the crew was waiting for. Kate switched the sound off for a moment. "Would anyone like to hear their message privately? The crew women looked around. By now, there were no secrets between them. Heads shook all around. "OK," she switched the sound on.

Kate's family was first. Her husband, Brian and son Donnie looked just the same until Brian told her about Donnie's 17th birthday party that was held just a month ago. When Kate had climbed into the ship, Donnie had not yet turned 16. Tears sprang to her eyes as she realized he would be 18 by the time she returned. She would never get those years back.

One by one, the crew heard from their loved ones. In minutes, there was the sound of snuffling and quiet sobbing as the women cried unabashedly over their long separations.

The cabin was quiet after the last transmission faded. Kate divided up the messages into individual segments and sent them to each crew woman's mailbox so they could view them again later.

"OK, crew. Let's get back to our posts, Jenir is next," she said softly.

It took a fourteen hours at impulse speed to reach Jenir, which had a very thin atmosphere. It was essentially a hunk of rock hurling through space.

"Looks a little like Mars," Greta said.

"Yeah, it does," agreed Kate. "Ready the probes. Maybe there will be some interesting minerals that NASA will find useful."

"Yeah, maybe it's made of gold," Beth smiled. "We could start a new gold rush out here."

Ally launched the probe and within a half-hour, the telemetry started flowing into the *Letanya's* databanks. The rock was composed mostly of iron ore, quartz and nickel.

Kate looked at the time. "All right, it's going to be another nine hours before we approach Castella. We've had a long day. Commander, set up a crew rotation. I know everyone's probably sick of sleeping, but we need to be alert when we check out these next two planets."

Tomorrow could be the day they make history, the crew thought as one.

Chapter 4

Castella, the fourth planet, was festooned with ice. Great floes bobbed in the oceans, sheets of ice covered the continents.

"Temperature is 9 degrees currently. And it's this planet's equivalent of high noon," Greta said, clearly disappointed.

"Well, that's a darn sight better than the minus 80 degrees we recorded last night," Kate said, looking at the monitor at the orb filling the screen.

The planet was beautiful — blue white and mysterious, its charms hidden beneath the ice. The *Letanya* sent down an explosive probe in an effort to reach the surface, but only succeeded in burrowing twenty feet into the glacier that covered the largest continent.

"Let's move on," Kate said suddenly. "Maybe we'll have more luck with Devon."

There was general agreement. Their mission was a huge success to date, yet the crew was vaguely disappointed. Four planets and none could support life. They were hoping for algae, plankton, amoeba — anything! Some new plant forms would be a welcome discovery.

"It's going to take us another three days to reach Devon at impulse speed," Kate said impulsively. "How about if we kick this thing in the ass and do a jump warp?"

Eyebrows were raised all around. A "jump warp" is definitely not recommended by NASA. It involves a short hop at warp speed to close distances quickly. It's equivalent to popping an aerocar into overdrive during a trip to the store.

Allyson was surprised by Kate's boldness. While Ally loved flying hot and fast when training on hyperjets back home, Kate was more conservative, an attribute that helped win her the captaincy. NASA doesn't let hot-shots fly their multi-billion-dollar spaceships.

"I'm impressed, captain," she said.

Kate reddened. "How much time could we save, commander?"

Ally did a quick calculation. "To bring us into position ten thousand kilometers from Devon, we'd need a, hmm, twelve-second warp."

Kate turned to the others. "What do you say—three days or twelve seconds?"

There was instant agreement. They'd all been too long in space to crawl along at impulse speed.

"OK, set it up. Let's strap in." Kate took her position, then looked around to make sure everyone else was secure. "No. 1, are you ready?"

"Aye, aye, sir."

"All right. Engage."

The stars blurred, an optical illusion created by warp drive. The ship shuddered for a moment, then the ride smoothed out as the ship hurled forward. Everyone hung on as if they were on a ride at Disney World, forgetting the fact that they had just spent seven months in warp. Being sound asleep helped.

Mentally, Kate counted off the seconds, then double-checked her guess when she reached ten. She looked down as the panel display ticked to ten—pretty close, she thought. The next two seconds seemed agonizingly slow.

The end of warp came with another shudder, the stars winked, then came into focus. The crew found themselves looking at Devon straight ahead as if it had suddenly appeared out of nowhere. It was a beautiful, blue-green and tan planet, full of promise.

"Check status!" Kate barked, worried that somehow, her impetuousness had endangered the mission.

"Green board," Ally responded immediately. "On course, ten thousand kilometers out, sir."

Kate breathed a sigh of relief and let her eyelids close briefly. "OK, let's man our stations. Looks like we have an excellent candidate here."

The *Letanya* sailed through the airless depths, closing fast on the mysterious sphere. The crew could see clouds over the mixture of sea and land. They all knew that clouds meant both rain and atmosphere, two vital components to life.

In a few minutes, they reached high orbit. "Launch probe," Kate said and Greta bent over the panel. A tiny vibration told them it was on its way.

Everyone held her breath as the probe rocketed down to the planet. It was designed to act like a missile until it reached the atmosphere, then fire retro-rockets to slow its descent. A parachute deploys at sixty thousand feet, allowing it to drift down, collecting data and radioing the information back to the ship.

"Chute deployed!" Greta sang out. "Telemetry coming in!"

Seconds dragged by. Kate wanted to shout at Greta to hurry up, but knew it always took the computer a little time to digest the information.

"Atmosphere—twenty-two percent oxygen, seventy-seven percent nitrogen!" Greta couldn't help but speak in exclamation points. The planet had breathable atmosphere—a stunning discovery. "Temperature, twenty-two degrees and rising!"

That was expected—the probe was still high up. "Humidity, seventeen percent." Greta was calmer now. She had the floor and enjoyed the feeling that everyone was listening with rapt attention.

"Thirty-one degrees. Probe is at forty thousand feet. Looks like it's going to be a warm day, sir."

That was true—if it's thirty degrees eight miles up, it could be rather hot at sea level. Perhaps even too hot for the away team. Still, Kate was encouraged by the data.

"Thirty thousand feet, thirty-nine degrees."

Everyone was on the edge of her seat now. The probes were designed to scan for lifeforms, but had a limited range. It had to drop below twenty-five thousand feet for large beings, and much lower for smaller ones. The silence stretched on.

"Twenty-five thousand, fifty degrees," Greta said, her eyes locked on the readout. Suddenly, she turned and looked around, eyes wide. "Lifeforms," she breathed. "Apparently mammalian. Large numbers. Many types."

There was a cheer, a sudden outburst of emotions that had been pent-up for months. Kate high-fived Ally, Beth hugged Jorja. The atmosphere was electric. Mammalian creatures breathed in oxygen and regulated their own temperature, just like the mammals of Earth. It was a huge discovery—far greater than any previous mission had discovered. Kate couldn't wait to send NASA the report on this finding.

Jorja broke in to the revelry. "Are we going to detonate?"

It was a sobering question. If any of these lifeforms were intelligent—a big if—the Prime Directive required that the crew detonate the probe before it could be spotted by any beings on the ground. Earthlings must not interfere with the development of another species and the idea of a strange, otherworldly object drifting down from the heavens could have unforeseen consequences. At a minimum, it would scare the crap out of them.

On the other hand, detonation robbed them of vital data closer to the ground. They hadn't established if the mammals were intelligent. It wouldn't matter to a bunch of cows, for example, if an object from space dropped into their midst. The problem is, they didn't know yet.

"Where will the probe fall?" Kate asked.

Greta looked up at another display screen. "Um. Land. Not far from a large group of mammals."

Kate shook her head. They could have allowed it to fall into the ocean, but not on land. Unless...

"What's the grouping of the mammals?" This was an important clue. If it's a herd, they would be grouped together for social interaction and protection against enemies. Intelligent beings tend to be more independent and thus are often spread out.

"Scattered," Greta replied. There was a murmur among the crew. She anticipated the next question. "Probe is hitting twenty-thousand feet."

"All right, give me a final temperature." Twenty thousand is about as low as NASA recommends. At four miles up, the sound would be minimal and debris would be well scattered. Much lower and you risk terrifying the residents.

"Sixty-two degrees."

"Hold a minute." Kate was acting on what everyone was thinking—just a few more seconds of data! NASA would not object to a detonation at a slightly lower altitude once they saw the results. "Let me know when we reach seventeen thousand."

Greta watched the screen. "Seventeen thousand."

"Detonate."

Greta pushed a button and the probe data vanished from her screen. "Probe destroyed at sixteen thousand, six hundred feet."

Kate nodded. Her euphoria over the discovery of life was tempered by the loss of data. "What was the final temperature?"

"Sixty-six degrees." Greta bent down and worked the numbers. "By my calculations, it should be close to ninety on the planet surface. Perfect sunbathing weather."

More good news. "All right, let's massage the data. Jorja, let's map the planet, starting from the area covered by the probe. Greta, let's coordinate the groupings of all lifeforms you recorded. Beth, see if you can add anything about these lifeforms. Ally, let's drop down into a lower orbit and get some detailed pictures."

The crew got to work, excited over their discoveries. Ally took the ship down to minimum orbit and focused the high-definition camera through her monitor. Her head snapped up. "Jesus," she breathed.

"Captain," she turned. "I think you're going to want to see this on the monitor."

"Switching over." Kate punched a button and the high-powered camera image jumped onto the large overhead monitor. Everyone's jaw fell open at once.

There were villages down below.

Chapter 5

Two hours later, they were poring over a map of the continents. A rough circle indicated where the probe had picked up lifeforms. Ally had a sheaf of photos taken of the area, plus others that showed several small towns grouped near water and forests.

"Here and here, two large groupings of the mammals that we can assume are intelligent," Greta was saying, pleased to have their attention. "And smaller ones here and here. Closer to the probe's drift radius, I picked up some scattered smaller mammals, and what appears to be reptilian lifeforms."

Reptiles too? It was beyond belief. This planet had evolved similar to Earth. The idea was staggering. Kate knew that this planet would soon be festooned with ships from Earth, all carrying scientists who would spend the rest of their lives discovering new facts about Devon.

Ally passed around the photos. "They have an agrarian society, probably similar to Earth of the fifteenth or sixteenth centuries. You can see they've tamed some beasts and use them to haul carts and plow fields."

Kate studied the photos. The beasts looked like donkeys, although they had thicker, shorter legs. The carts rode on large wooden wheels. In one photo, she could see a cage of some sort over one of the carts. Probably transporting prisoners, she mused, which would indicate some sort of judicial system. This world fascinated her.

"The beings in these villages are humanoid, not all that dissimilar from us. I've asked the computer to develop a more accurate picture of both sexes, based on what we can see from here." She pushed some buttons and small holograms appeared before them on the flat top of the display.

Two creatures appeared, standing side by side and rotating slowly. They were darker, with more body hair, but otherwise looked human. Both had two arms and legs, a face with two eyes, a nose and mouth. The woman had two breasts. The only obvious differences were in the foreheads and ears. A narrow, lumpy bone extended down from the hairline to the bridge of the nose and the ears were flatter and attached to the skull.

The average man appeared to be larger and more powerful than a human male. The man's chest was deep and well developed, indicating hard work. The woman looked much the same as an Earth woman, except she had some scattering of hair between her breasts, as well as the expected hair in her armpits, on legs and pubis.

Because of the apparent heat on the surface, the humanoid images wore hardly any clothes at all. The woman was entirely naked, except for animal skins wrapped around her feet. The man wore a covering over his privates as well as foot skins.

Jorja spoke right up. "Let's see what the computer can do without the clothes." Everyone smiled.

Kate sighed. "Well, I suppose, as long as it's in the interest of science. Computer, can you generate an image of the male being without clothes?"

"Insufficient data," the metallic voice intoned.

"Damn!" Jorja said.

"Why are the women naked?" Beth asked.

Ally shrugged. "Maybe it's custom."

"The men sure look strong," Jorja said. *She needs to go off somewhere and masturbate*, Kate thought.

It did give her an idea. "Computer, replace the female image with that of an average human male."

The woman vanished and the image of a naked man appeared. Compared to the native, the Earth man looked like a ninety-pound weakling. "Scale," Kate said. A scale rose up next to the holograms. The Earthling was six feet tall. The native was easily six-six and probably outweighed him by fifty pounds or more.

"Wow," Beth said. "Look how they've developed. Makes us look puny in comparison."

"Let's compare the women too."

Kate gave the instructions and in seconds, holograms of a native woman and an Earth woman appeared side by side. The scale showed the native was only about two inches taller than the average Earth woman, who stood five-six, according to the scale.

"They're a lot like us, only hairier," Greta put in.

"Yeah, a *lot* hairier," Jorja said. Everyone laughed. On Earth, American custom dictated that women remove all their body hair, a trend that had begun around the beginning of the 21st century. The development of depilatories had advanced to the point to where women entering puberty could use them to kill the hair roots, leaving their skin silky smooth.

Kate brought up the native pair as before, and the crew just stared at the images for a few minutes.

"God, this is such a huge discovery," Jorja said. "We're going to be famous."

"Too bad we can't name the planet after you," Beth said to Kate.

"Maybe they could name the humanoids after you," Greta put in. "Welcome to the planet of the Dysons." The crew laughed and Kate laughed right along with them.

"Let's get some more data," she said. "I want to launch another probe, only this time, over water. See if we can get it close to land, but not too close. I'd like to record some ocean temperatures, salinity, et cetera."

They had to wait fifteen minutes for the planet to circle around underneath them before they could launch. There had been some discussion about where the next probe should be sent. The obvious choice would be to launch the next one on the other side of the planet to see if lifeforms existed everywhere. Greta had a better suggestion—launch a probe near where the first one fell in order collect more detailed data in anticipation of a manned landing. She would lead it, of course.

Kate agreed. She knew NASA would insist upon exploring the planet, provided they could avoid contact with the beings.

The probe burrowed through the atmosphere, on target to a splashdown about ten miles offshore, four-hundred kilometers east of the first probe. The footprints of the two probes would overlap, giving them an excellent view of climate conditions and geological topography as well as additional information about the humanoids.

"Chute deployed!" Greta sang out. "Telemetry coming in!"

The initial data was similar to that collected by the first probe. The crew waited for the probe to fall below twenty thousand feet.

"Fifteen thousand. Wind, thirty knots! Temperature sixty-eight degrees!" A few seconds passed. "Ten thousand, seventy-five degrees."

"Hot and windy—a dangerous combination," Ally said.

"Five thousand, eight-eight degrees...Gravity, zero-point-nine-two of Earth. One thousand, ninety-two degrees. Wind, sixteen knots."

"No wonder they don't wear clothes. Do you think it ever gets colder there?" Beth put in.

"I'm sure our scientists will find that out. The system will be swarming with them within a year," Kate responded.

"Splashdown! Ocean water temperature is ... fifty-nine degrees. Salinity is ninety-four percent saltwater, plus trace elements." Greta looked up. "None appear to be harmful to humans. I'm also reading lifeforms below the surface.

"We have a very livable planet."

Big grins jumped to their faces. Kate knew it was time to report in.

"Ladies, let's phone home."

Chapter 6

To say NASA was stunned would be an understatement. After Kate radioed in their lengthy report, it took an agonizing two-and-a-half hours for them to respond, longer than any of the crew expected.

"They must have fainted," Greta suggested.

"Yeah, or they're trying to figure out how to steal the glory from us 'girls,'" Jorja said, getting a dark look from the captain.

"Message coming in!" Ally intoned. Everyone's head swiveled around to the screen.

"Onscreen," Kate ordered.

John Philips appeared, with James Hunter standing right behind him. "Congratulations, crew of the *Letanya*!" Phillips said. "We received your message, plus some of the supporting documents, and I can tell you, we are absolutely blown away by the discovery. I'm sure you—"

Hunter thrust his face into the camera, elbowing Phillips aside.

Typical, thought Kate.

"Ladies, I'm sure you can appreciate the magnitude of your discovery," he said. "The news is just now beginning to break here, and it's getting a tremendous response. CNN is devoting the rest of the afternoon to the *Letanya*, and what the findings might mean for us.

"The most shocking aspect of this discovery, as I'm sure you've contemplated, is how such similar beings developed more than two million light years apart. We've already decided to send our next ship, the *Sovereign*, to the Denoba system to further the exploration." Kate recalled that the *U.S.S. Sovereign*, still under construction, had been scheduled to explore the Milky Way. To make such a sudden switch showed how important their discoveries were to NASA.

"Naturally, we're giving you permission to head down to the planet surface for a closer study of the creatures, provided, of course, that you don't make contact with them. I'm sure you're well aware of the Prime Directive."

Kate didn't need to be reminded. And she doubted he would've said the same thing to an all-male crew, but maybe she was just being sensitive.

"The decision to go below is yours, Capt. Dyson, we don't want you to risk your overall mission. But I can assure you, the people of Earth are going crazy over this news and want more details. If you can collect some better photographs, plus some plant species that would be a tremendous boon to our knowledge of Devon planet and people.

"Please keep in close contact for the next few days. Even little scraps of information will be anxiously awaited here." Hunter looked to his left. "OK, I'm going to return you to Phillips, who has some mission parameters to discuss."

Hunter vanished from the screen and Kate found herself breathing a little sigh of relief. The welcomed face of the mission controller appeared, looking unruffled at being pushed aside.

"*Letanya*, I'm back," Phillips said, deadpan. The crew chuckled. "Now, regulations require that I go over this checklist, although I know you are all well-trained in planet landings."

That was partially true—the crew had landed dozens of times in simulators, but only three times on Earth, after being launched from an orbiting shuttle. It's one thing to land on your home planet, but quite another to land in a possibly inhospitable, unknown world. The risks were considerable.

The *Letanya* was equipped with two identical "shuttle pods," each approximately twenty feet in length, with a pair of stubby wings extending out from the undercarriage. Each can hold three crewmen, sitting one behind the other. Because of the way they appear, the pods are nicknamed "bobsleds" by the crew. With the big engine at the rear, they actually look a lot more like rocket cars of the late 20th century.

Phillips outlined what problems the pilot—Greta, in this case—might encounter due to the high winds recorded at around twenty thousand feet. The stubby wings aren't enough to provide the stability necessary at lower altitudes, so Greta would pull a lever to deploy wing extensions that would give them a longer glide. Thrusters help control speed of descent and direction.

It was important not to fire the main engine once the craft enters the atmosphere, as there's limited fuel. Burn too much on the way down and you'll never reach the spaceship again.

Greta, Kate observed, was following Phillips directions carefully, her face glowing with the knowledge that she would soon be landing on the surface of a brave new world. Kate wondered if she was already imagining her ticker-tape parade.

The transmission ended and everyone just sat for a few minutes, taking it all in. Kate could see similar expressions on the faces of Beth and Jorja, who would make up the other away team members.

Kate felt it was time to sober them up. "I still haven't decided if a surface mission is a good idea," she said. Heads snapped around.

"Here are my concerns." She ticked them off her fingers. "One, we can learn a lot from continued observation from orbit. It may be far more valuable to return safely to Earth with all our data intact than to risk everything on a limited venture to the planet. Two, we're out here two million light years away, completely on our own. If something goes wrong, no one can come to our aid. We don't know what to expect on the surface in the way of plants, animals or even microbes. We could bring something aboard that may be harmful. Three, we run a real risk of accidentally coming into contact with the natives. That could cause ripple effects in their development we have no way of anticipating. It also could introduce diseases that could devastate them — or us."

The eyes of the crew were wide. They knew every word the captain said was true. But would she really overrule them and make them go home without a surface exploration?

"But we've come so far —" Greta began. Kate held up a hand.

"I know, I know. I'm fully aware of what Houston said and how history will judge us. If we returned to Earth without exploring, we'll be seen as timid women who were afraid to take risks. But if something goes wrong, we'll be seen as impulsive women who took unnecessary chances. Either way, we're screwed.

"Now, just like you, I didn't come all this way to meekly go home without seeing what awaits us down below. But if we're going to do this, it's going to be done by the book. We're going to triple-check everything. We're going to abort if anything, and I mean anything, goes wrong. I'm not going to risk the crew or the humanoids or even the smallest life on the planet."

"We wouldn't want to either, captain," Greta said, grateful that Kate seemed to be leaning toward approving the landing.

"I want us to find the best spot for a landing," Kate continued. "It must allow plenty of room for a soft landing. It should be well away from a village, but perhaps close enough to hike to in order to observe the residents. It needs to provide camouflage for the bobsled. If we can't find such a site, we don't go. Before we launch, I want a bio-probe sent down to the landing site to check for microbes, poisonous plants, vicious animals — you name it. If we find anything like that, we don't go."

Heads nodded. They were like children, trying to convince Mom to let them walk to a neighbor's house. *We'll be good, we'll stay on the sidewalk, we won't talk to strangers!*

Kate looked each of the three away team members in their eyes, telling them silently how important this is. "OK. Let's get busy."

The next few hours were a blur of activity. Sites were explored, then rejected for one reason or another. Finally, the crew narrowed down the list to three possible landing sites. The captain went over each site carefully, looking for flaws, dangers.

"Site One is about 10 klicks from this village, on the other side of a forest," Greta was explaining, using the shorthand for kilometers. "We can put in at night, hide the ship, then hike over and set up a base camp near the edge of the woods."

Kate shook her head. "They'll spot you coming in. When you fire your thrusters, you'll light up the sky."

"Maybe we could come in 'hot'," she said, then instantly regretted her words.

"That's the kind of thinking that will get this mission cancelled," Kate shot back. "You either land by the book or you don't land at all, got it?"

Greta nodded, chagrined.

"Here's another possibility that solves the problem of being seen as we land," Jorja put in, anxious to move on.

"Site Two," Greta picked up, pointing to the topography map, "is here, at the beginning of this mountain range. See, these two ridges rise out of the desert, then join to form a larger ridge. At the junction, the woods begin. We can fly in and land safely on the sand between the two ridges, then slid up to near the treeline. Using harnesses, we can drag the bobsled into the woods for cover."

Greta handed Kate a photo of the site. "On the other side of this range, across this plain, is a small village. We figure we can climb the ridge here—it's not too high at this point—and set up base camp near the top. With long-range scanners and binoculars, we can observe the people without being spotted. The village would be about five kilometers away."

"What about the U.T.?" Kate asked. The Universal Translator was a key part of this mission. The U.T., often pronounced "Ute," was a modification of the devices typically found on Earth that travelers use when visiting another country. About the size of a deck of playing cards, the device instantly translates speech into the desired language. Of course, all of Earth's languages have been studied and recorded. Dealing with a brand new language requires a considerable learning curve. The U.T. must be allowed to record at least an hour of continuous language in order to formulate a working translation. The away team would have to get close enough to place microphone-transmitters — a risky and dangerous business.

Greta knew that Kate wanted to hear how they'd solve this problem. "Jorja has manufactured some 'rocks' in which we can hide the mics," she said. "Two of us will sneak up in the middle of the night and place them close enough to listen in. Then we can just sit back and record."

"Sounds risky. How can you avoid being spotted?"

"We've talked about that. There's a ravine here," Greta pointed to the photo, "that will allow us to get pretty close. Then we'll come out here and place a rock near the western edge of the village, near this road."

"You'd be exposed for a hundred yards or more. That's too risky. You'll stand out like sore thumbs."

"Um, we have a solution for that as well, sir," Beth spoke up for the first time. "We'll simply disguise ourselves as natives, out collecting wood or something."

Kate's brow furrowed. "That means —" She couldn't finish.

"Yes, we'll have to be naked or dressed in animal skins. We'll have to make our bodies look, um, more native."

Kate laughed out loud at the image that created in her mind. "You're going to *add* hair?"

"Only enough to get by at night, from a distance," Greta added quickly. "A strip here, a patch there. We'll put them on just before we plant the rocks. We don't expect to be seen at all. This will just be an added precaution."

The captain nodded. They certainly had thought this out. "OK, let's check out the third site."

That site was soon rejected for the same reasons as the first—it was too exposed. Kate gave them approval to further explore Site Two.

A bioprobe was launched in the middle of the night. The bioprobes are much smaller than regular probes and thus are harder to spot. Just a few hundred meters up, a small chute deploys, allowing it to drift to the ground.

The probe was aimed well. It drifted across the sand and landed in a tree about a mile from where the away team hoped to drag their bobsled. "Signal coming in," Greta called out. She scanned the reports. "No poisonous plants, no microbes and no dangerous animals or insects in the immediate vicinity," she announced after several seconds. "I'll continue to scan."

A sigh of relief went up from Beth and Jorja. Even the captain nodded. "All right. I'll call it in. Looks like we have a 'go.'"

Chapter 7

NASA was as excited about the upcoming launch as the away team. Hunter wanted a full report as soon as the team touched down, then regular reports every three hours. "You have no idea of the magnitude of the news here at home," he gushed. "It's on the news every day. They've started a cable channel just for the *Letanya*. Why, there was a baby girl born right here in Houston yesterday and the parents named her Letanya — can you believe it?"

Kate had trouble understanding all the hoopla. They were just doing their jobs.

Greta took over the preparation of the shuttle and crew. Kate and Allyson stood by like mother hens, nervously looking for loopholes in their planning. Greta rolled her eyes at her team when the commanders weren't looking.

All too soon, they were ready to go. They had food and water for a week, though the mission was to last just three days. Beth inserted a subcutaneous tracking module the size of a match into the upper arms of each of them. It would allow the *Letanya* to pinpoint their positions at all times.

Each woman carried a U.T. and a spare radio in the pockets of their overalls for triple redundancy. The rest of the gear had been loaded and double-checked.

Kate handed each woman a small phase pistol, to be used only in emergencies, she warned them. To ensure that the pistols did not fall into the hands of the natives, they included a unique design. A small square halfway down the grip on both sides accepted the middle finger of a user, whether using the phaser left-handed or right. A scanner read the fingerprint. If it didn't match the assigned user, the phaser remained inert. If a member of the away team needed to switch weapons for some reason, she would have to hold the gun, then punch in a five-digit code at the base of the grip to reprogram the scanner.

The team got dressed in their bulky spacesuits. The backpacks wouldn't be needed — just a spare oxygen bottle was carried in case the pod's system failed. That meant, of course, the women couldn't urinate in the suits.

"Be sure and pee before you go, gals, 'cause we aren't stopping at a gas station on the way," joked Greta.

Beth packed her medical kit behind her seat. Kate and Ally helped the team into the pod. Greta in front, Jorja behind her and Beth taking up the rear seat. The commanders helped strap them in and connect their hoses to the ship's air-conditioning and oxygen supplies. When they were ready for the helmets, Kate paused to grip Greta's shoulder. With a nod of her head, Kate indicated the other pod, sitting on the other side of the chamber. "Be very careful. Don't make us come down there and get you, OK?"

Greta nodded, the bravado scared out of her as the launch approached. "Don't worry, sir. We'll make America proud of us."

Kate nodded, then eased the helmet over the woman's head. Once all were locked down and gave the thumbs up, Kate and Ally lowered the long canopy. They left the launch chamber, dogging down the door carefully behind them.

Making their way forward, they lowered themselves into the bridge chairs and checked the radio. "*Letanya* calling Eagle One, can you read me?"

"Roger, *Letanya*. Loud and clear."

"Prepare for launch sequence."

Kate checked the board. Everything seemed clear. She looked over at Ally. She nodded. Kate pressed the button to launch countdown.

Inside the pod, the women sat rigid. The experience reminded Beth of waiting for the roller coaster ride to start. Only this one had no rails or safety nets. The air whooshed out of the chamber. The bay door slid open noiselessly beneath them. They were too confined to peek at the planet below. They hung there, over nothingness, held only by the launch grappler.

"Ten, nine, eight..."

Greta ran through her procedures, trying to ignore her fear. *This is my big test*, she told herself. *Don't blow it.*

"Pod released." The away team felt the sickening lurch as the grappler pushed the pod clear of the ship, then released it. The pod drifted down for a few seconds, then the main engine kicked in, rocketing them toward the rim of the planet.

Kate and Ally watched their trajectory. "On course. End burn in six seconds." She counted down. "End burn."

Greta cut the engine, keeping an eye on their position. It was critical to enter the atmosphere at precisely the right angle. Too flat and they'd skip off and have to abort the mission. Too steep and they'd burn up before they reached thicker air.

Greta let the computer steer the craft. Her turn would come soon enough. In seconds, they felt the first vibrations from the thickening atmosphere.

"Entering atmosphere. About to lose radio contact."

"Roger. See you on the other side," Kate responded. This would be the most nerve-wrenching part of the trip. They would have to wait to see if they made it.

Sparks flew up outside the canopy. The ride became rougher. The women hung on, praying silently that all of NASA's engineering prowess would be enough to keep them alive for the trip.

The outside was a whirl of sparks, heat, and gas. Beth turned up her suit's air conditioning to full and watched the temperature gauge inside the shuttle climb even as she felt cooler.

The trip through the upper atmosphere took just nine minutes, but it seemed like an hour to the away team. Finally, they noticed a lessening of the heat wave outside, then blue sky and clouds.

" —anya, come in, Eagle One," burst through their headphones.

"Eagle One here, *Letanya*. All systems go." Greta replied coolly, as if she did this sort of thing every day.

"Good to hear your voice. You are on track for landing."

The pod was still in daylight here. As they fell and the planet rotated under them, they would soon enter the darkest part of the night. With luck, they could glide in to a dead-stick landing and not need retro-rockets at all.

Right now, the pod was a hot brick falling from a great height. Greta counted down the time to deploy the wing extensions. "Deploying wings," she radioed. The extensions folded out smoothly. The ship began behaving more like a plane now. Greta banked it back and forth slightly, getting the feel of it. Behind her, Beth and Jorja blanched.

"Watch for turbulence below thirty thousand feet," Kate radioed.

Greta checked her altimeter. Thirty six thousand and falling. She checked her course and speed. A little fast, but not too bad. Down, down they flew, the clouds swirling around them.

The first turbulence hit them like a fist, jerking them in their seats. The power of the wind startled the mission commander. She had experienced many rough rides before, but this was sudden and severe. Beth felt a warm splash of urine soak her panties. *You're scaring the piss out of me, Greta!*

Grimly, Greta set her jaw and hung on to the controls. More air blasts jerked them around. They drifted off course, and Greta correctly immediately, pleased that the pod responded quickly.

"Eagle One, watch your heading. Your speed is dropping as well."

"Roger, *Letanya*. We're rocking and rolling down here." Greta wished the captain would leave her alone for a few minutes.

Kate was worried. "This turbulence is worse than we thought," she told Ally. The commander just nodded. There was nothing that could be said.

Greta watched the altimeter: Twenty thousand, fifteen thousand. *Come on, baby! Let's get through this!* Another big jolt rocked them and Greta was shocked to see a red light flash on her console. The forward thruster was offline! She thumbed the diagnostics switch and held her breath, hoping the problem was a bad relay or display light. The light went yellow for a few seconds, then returned to red. "Damn!"

"Eagle One, Eagle One. We see a red light here. Confirm."

"Roger, *Letanya*, we've lost forward thrusters. Will compensate."

Kate didn't like it. Losing the forward retro-rocket meant the pod could not be slowed except by raising the nose. And that would lengthen the glide path. Considering that the pod was heading into the base of a mountain, expecting to land short, a longer glide path could be disastrous. The captain had to rely on Greta's skills to land the shuttle safely.

The pod broke through ten thousand feet and the turbulence began to diminish. Greta regained control and flew on, adjusting the pitch minutely when the speed peaked above flight norms. She felt her confidence returning.

"Eagle One to *Letanya*, we've broken through the turbulence layer and have smooth sailing ahead."

"Roger, Eagle One," Kate didn't like the cocky attitude she heard. Then again, maybe Greta was just trying to reassure everyone. *God knows we could use that!*

Greta felt much better. They were nearing the landing zone, so she slipped her night vision goggles on and let the heads-up display jump before her eyes. She could see they were right on the glide path, and just nine knots fast. She raised the nose a bit to reduce speed and watched as the pod came up out of the glide path. She would have to porpoise the ship from now on, dipping below the glide path until the speed rose too quickly, then coming up to cut speed and get back on glide.

She had rehearsed just such a problem many times on the simulator. *Piece of cake,* she thought. The ship dropped below seven thousand and Greta looked ahead to spot the landing site. The mountain range appeared. She magnified it for a moment to look for cloud cover or other problems. It looked clear.

Dipping down, the pod came in on its final approach. *It would be exhilarating,* Jorja thought, *if I wasn't so terrified.*

Greta tested the forward thruster, just to make sure it was out. The computer had not lied to her. Side thrusters showed green, but she didn't need them now. Her speed was still a bit too high. She thought she might be able to raise the nose one more time to cut speed before she had to lock in on the glide plane. Greta pulled back on the stick and heard the glide alarm sound, even as the speed dropped below 115 knots.

Above, Kate was alarmed to see her display indicate the pod was porpoising, but she wisely did not call Greta. The mission commander did not need to hear from her captain right now. She needed to fly.

Greta punched the intercom. "Team, we're coming in a little hot. I'll let you know when to brace."

Jorja and Beth felt their hearts race at the news. They put their trust in Greta's skill—after all, what else could they do?

The ground loomed up at them. Greta flew this crate like she used to fly jump jets through the canyons of Utah. She found herself actually grinning as the pod raced through the night. She loved control and this small emergency would make her even more heroic once they landed safely. And she had no doubt that they would.

"*Letanya*, Eagle One making final approach. Hang on."

"Roger." Kate didn't want to say anything else. Unconsciously, she crossed her fingers.

"Brace yourselves," Greta said calmly, just before the pod touched down. Initially, the landing was textbook, a beautiful display of skill and grace. The commander put it down right where she had to in order to slide to a stop safely short of the treeline. If there had been any problem, she could have fired her front thrusters to slow the craft, but that was impossible now. The craft landed softly and began its slide and it looked as if Greta had pulled it off.

Then the craft hit a partially submerged boulder and was bounced up into the air for a few dozen feet. The sudden lack of resistance changed the friction coefficient. Instead of coasting to a stop, the pod slid fifty feet further, into the tree line. There was nothing Greta could do. The nose of the pod thudded hard against a tree, cracking the trunk and causing it to topple over slowly onto the pod.

Silence settled over the scene.

Chapter 8

"*Letanya*, calling Eagle One, *Letanya*, calling Eagle One." Kate was frantic. Telemetry was cut off within seconds of touching down and now she couldn't raise them. Did they crash? It couldn't be. Not them, not now. She repeated her radio call.

Ally came over to stand next the captain. "Tracking devices show them to be right where they should be."

Kate nodded. The devices would work whether the team was dead or alive, so it was small comfort.

"Should I prepare the second pod?"

"No, not yet. We'll follow regs on this." NASA wisely didn't want rescue missions being taken prematurely. Give the away team a chance to radio in. They had plenty of back-ups, after all, Kate thought.

Unless they're all dead.

She pushed the thought out of her mind. *Shit!* Everything was going so well, too.

Down on the planet, Beth groaned and opened her eyes. When the pod hit the tree, her helmet had rocked forward, causing her to black out momentarily. Fortunately, the seat straps had protected her from being flung into Jorja's seat.

She keyed the intercom. "Jorja? Commander?" Beth reached up and touched Jorja's shoulder. The woman stirred. Beth saw her fumble for her mic switch. "Doc? You OK?"

"Yeah, you?"

"Yes, just a little groggy. Hang on, I'll check on the commander." Beth watched as Jorja leaned forward and shook the inert form ahead of her. Greta didn't move.

"OK, I need to get out and check on her. Help me raise the canopy."

The tree branches made it impossible to use the internal hydraulics to raise the glass. Jorja and Beth pushed together and managed to open it about eighteen inches before it fell back into place. "Shit," Beth said. "I need something to prop it open with." She looked around. There was nothing, of course.

Wait! Their helmets! Beth unstrapped herself from the seat, then twisted the helmet off. "Jorja," she tapped on her shoulder. "Take your helmet off and we'll use them."

Jorja nodded and soon they were both able to talk freely. "OK, raise it up and slide them into place." They strained to push back against the branches. Then, with their left hands, they pushed the helmets into position. The canopy gaped open just enough for Beth to squeeze through.

Standing next to the crippled pod, Beth shrugged out of her bulky spacesuit. Even in the middle of the night it was too hot. Beth unzipped the NASA coveralls down to her navel, then went to the front of the pod and checked on Greta. The commander was unconscious, her faceplate shattered. Blood dripped from her face.

"We've got to get her out of there," she told Jorja. "Hang on, I'm going to phase some of these branches."

Jorja nodded. The emergency the captain had warned them about had already arrived. The phasers would be necessary. Beth found a couple of branches that pressed down on the canopy and cut them away. The blue-white light lit up the night like a welding torch. Beth hated to use it. She carefully reset the phaser on stun when she was finished.

With the canopy clear, Jorja was able to scramble out. She immediately stripped off her hot suit, but she didn't stop there. "I'm burning up," she explained as she unzipped her coveralls and stepped clear. Now she was just dressed in a tee-shirt, bra and panties. Beth thought she looked much more comfortable. Her own coveralls were hot too. She wanted to take them off, but first she had to attend to Greta. Beth got the medical kit from the rear of the pod.

"Hang on, I'll scan her." Both women approached the commander. Beth waved the device over Greta's inert body. "Broken nose, concussion and a sprained left knee. Shit." The concussion could be a problem, depending on how severe it was. "We're going to have to protect that knee when we get her out," she told the engineer.

They left her helmet on to protect Greta's head. Beth got an inflate-cast from the kit. She reached down and carefully placed it around the woman's knee. It was an awkward reach. She inflated the cast, pulled back and nodded to Jorja.

The larger woman was a tremendous help in pulling Greta free. Beth supported her legs. Soon they had her on the ground. Beth removed the helmet and examined her wounds. She had a gash between her eyebrows where she had been cut by the faceplate. The bridge of her nose appeared slightly discolored and askew. Her nose bled. Beth gingerly pulled it back into position. Greta groaned but did not wake up.

Beth checked out her leg. The scan showed no tears to the ligaments, for which she was grateful. It would be stiff and sore for a few days, maybe longer. The concussion was another matter. Greta shouldn't be unconscious this long. Quickly, she used a clean cloth from her kit and water from her canteen to wash Greta's wounds.

Turning to Jorja, Beth said, "We have to get her back to the ship."

Jorja nodded. "I'll check out the damage to the pod."

"I'll try to raise the captain." Beth took the back-up radio out of her coveralls. "*Letanya*, this is Eagle One. *Letanaya*, this is Eagle One. Come in, please."

Aboard the *Letanya*, Kate and Ally were pacing, hoping that the crew survived whatever had happened down there. When the radio crackled to life, they both jumped for the controls. Kate got there first.

"Eagle One, this is *Letanya*! Go ahead!" Kate couldn't keep her worry and frantic desperation out of her voice.

"This is Dr. Reyes. We've crash-landed on the planet, sir. The commander is injured and needs immediate evacuation. Smith is checking out the pod."

Kate closed her eyes, her worst fears realized.

"Eagle One, are you and Smith all right?"

"Roger."

"What is the extent of the commander's injuries?"

Beth described them, then looked up as Jorja approached. "Hang on, captain, I'll let the engineer describe the damage to the pod." She handed over the radio.

"Smith here, captain. The bobsled is heavily damaged. I may be able to repair it, given the right replacement parts, but I won't know for awhile."

Kate closed her eyes again and pinched the bridge of her nose. She had so wanted everything to go smoothly. Now her crew was trapped on the planet and Hunter was waiting for a report.

She keyed the mic. "All right, I will be sending Commander Egerton down..." She looked at her watch and realized they could not send down the other pod in the time they had left before daylight. "...tomorrow night. Send us a list of parts you need. Egerton will return with Hanson and Reyes, then come back to help you. Acknowledge."

"Roger that. We'll be in touch."

"Oh, and Eagle One?"

"Yes, sir?"

"Stay out of sight, close to the pod. I'm aborting the away mission."

"Roger. Out."

Kate turned to Ally. "That last order was probably obvious."

Ally nodded. "But it had to be said. For the record."

"Speaking of which. I have a phone call to make."

"I don't envy you this one, captain."

Chapter 9

Jorja and Beth put on the harnesses and managed to pull the pod free of the tree. Jorja set to work, taking apart the crushed nose casing, trying to determine what needed repair or replacement. Beth wanted to take the hot spacesuit off of Greta. She had already stripped off her hot coveralls, and now was dressed like Jorja, in just a tee-shirt, bra and panties.

Slowly, the night gave way to dawn. Beth had managed to get the spacesuit and the coveralls off of Greta. Now she wore a tee-shirt and panties. No bra. *Showoff,* Beth thought. Greta still had not awakened. Beth scanned her head again, looking for anything she may have missed, but found nothing new. She had better equipment aboard the ship that might give her a clue.

She looked up as Jorja approached. The engineer looked dejected. "What's the story?"

"It's junk. The outer skin is cracked, which means we need a titanium welder to get it space-worthy again."

"Shit." There was no such equipment on board the *Letanya* due to weight considerations.

"You got that right."

They sat dejectedly for a few minutes.

Greta groaned. The two women froze and turned toward her. Beth was beside the commander in a flash. "Greta? Commander?"

Greta opened her eyes and squinted against the dawn light. "Ouch." She turned away. Beth let her shadow fall over her.

"Here, have some water." Beth let a little trickle into her mouth. Greta coughed, but drank it down. "Do you remember what happened?"

Greta shook her head, then groaned from the pain that caused her. "No. Am I on the ship?"

"No. We're still on the planet surface. We need to get you back."

The commander opened her eyes. "We landed?"

"Yes."

"How did we get here? Who flew the pod?"

"You did." Beth looked over at Jorja, worry etched on her face. "You did a good job, but you hit your head when we landed."

"I flew?" Greta was groggy. "I landed?" She clearly had no recollection of anything that had happened since they left the *Letanya*. "Help me sit up."

"That's not a good idea, commander. You've have a bad concussion. You need to rest."

Greta didn't argue, which told Beth a lot about the woman's head injury. It wasn't like her to accept advice, even from her doctor. In another few minutes, she had passed out again.

"Well, I guess we'd better call and give the bad news."

"Yeah. The captain isn't going to like it." Beth wet a cloth and placed it on Greta's head.

"*Shit!*"

Beth looked up at Jorja, surprised to hear the sudden exclamation from the normally cool and calm engineer.

Jorja was looking off to Beth's left. She turned her head and was so surprised, she sat down suddenly on her haunches, the breath forced out of her.

There was a humanoid standing between the trees, about 40 feet away, watching them. He seemed as shocked as they were. He was a big man, easily six-foot-six. Beth guessed that he weighed 275 pounds. Back home, he'd be a football player nicknamed "Lumpy" or "Bubba." Like the holographic image they had seen, he wore only a loincloth. Animal skins covered his feet. His chest was hairy, his legs and arms less so.

Lumpy grunted something the women could not understand. His thick brow furrowed. He took a step forward, grunted again and made a sweeping gesture with his arm.

Beth caught a movement out of the corner of her eye and turned to see Jorja pulling her phaser from the pile of discarded coveralls. "Jorja," she warned.

"I'd say this constitutes an emergency, wouldn't you?"

Perhaps, she thought. But stunning one of them will probably just make things worse. "I don't think that's going to help."

"Well, I'm not going to be murdered, either. Get on the radio and call for the pod. I don't think we should wait for nightfall anymore."

Beth nodded. She stood slowly and backed away. The creature just stared at her, as if trying to figure out who these strange beings were. He took another step toward them and Jorja raised her pistol. "Don't come any closer," she warned.

The humanoid stopped, as if confused by Jorja's strange words.

Beth found the radio and called the ship. "Eagle One, calling *Letanya*, Eagle One calling *Letanya*!" She fought panic. They were in deep trouble. They faced a Hobson's choice and no matter how it turns out, they would have still violated the Prime Directive. "Hunter is going to run us out of NASA," she said aloud without realizing it.

"Eagle One, this is *Letanya*, go ahead."

"Captain, we've got a situation here."

Then all hell broke loose. The humanoid took another step toward Jorja, who pointed the weapon and seemed ready to fire, when suddenly, she cried out and the pistol fell from her hand. Beth looked over and saw a second humanoid, just as tall but more slender, stepping out from the trees to Jorja's right. He held something in his hand. *What the hell? They aren't supposed to have sophisticated weapons!*

"Go ahead, Eagle One."

Beth raised the radio and the humanoid flicked his arm. A rock struck her fingers, knocking the radio from her hand. "Ow! Shit!" She danced around, holding her fingers. Jorja dove for her pistol and the creature flicked another rock, striking her on the head. She collapsed.

"Eagle One, come in."

Beth dropped down and crawled to the coveralls, trying to uncover her phase pistol. The humanoids were closing in on her. Greta sat up, confused. She looked around and saw their attackers, but it didn't seem to register. "Who are you?" she said.

"Eagle One, please come in. Eagle One."

Beth's hand grasped the pistol. She brought it up, aimed at the rock-throwing man and pulled the trigger. Nothing happened. With sudden horror, Beth realized she had picked up Greta's phaser by mistake. Before she could find her weapon, the slender man ran up and backhanded her across the head. She fell dazed.

"Eagle One, come in!"

Chapter 10

"Dammit!" Kate slammed her hand down on the console. "What the hell happened?"

"Whatever it was, it overcame them quickly. I had the scanners focused on that area and we would've been able to pick up phaser blasts. There was nothing."

"Eagle One, this is *Letanya*, come in, dammit!" Kate knew she was losing control and sucked in a deep breath.

Her call home a short time ago had brought the reaction she had expected. Mindful of Hunter's warning back on Earth, Kate simply told Houston the pod was on the surface and they were awaiting word of their discoveries. It was a short message and Kate knew it wouldn't fool Hunter for a moment.

His reply—coming exactly one hour and forty-two minutes later, indicating an instant response—was laced with criticism.

"Your last message leaves a lot to be desired, captain," he said, his face set. "The president, along with Congress, have cancelled their meetings for the rest of the day in order to sit by the phone or the TV to hear each of your reports. I've got reporters from 146 countries camped outside my office. I want much more detail than you've been willing to give us. Just exactly what is going on out there? What aren't you telling us?"

Kate wasn't sure what to do. If she told Houston what had happened, it would set up exactly the scenario Hunter had warned her about. If she tried to lie or whitewash the situation, her career would be over and history would never forgive her.

She knew she'd have to play it by the book. Tell them what's happened and let NASA sort it out.

"Uh, captain." Ally was bent over the scope.

Kate didn't really want to hear any more bad news. "Yeah?"

Ally looked up. "The away team is on the move."

"What! They had orders to stay by the pod, so if they're moving, they've just violated my direct or —"

"Or they're not going of their own free will," Ally said quietly.

Kate closed her eyes. "Get the camera onscreen."

In seconds, they were looking at the landing site, covered with trees. "Overlay the transponder signals." Three yellow dots appeared, close together, among the trees. Kate watched with morbid fascination. If they were moving under their own power, they were sure going slow.

"Reyes' report said the commander had a badly sprained knee, right? Maybe they're helping her to walk," Kate said, grasping at straws.

"It's possible. But why would they leave the pod?"

"Perhaps an environmental situation? Some sort of hazard?"

"They would've told us, sir. No, what happened to them was sudden and overwhelming."

"You don't think —"

"One way to find out."

Kate nodded. "OK, let's send a bioprobe right down on their heads, see if we can pick up any humanoid readings."

"And we thought we were in trouble with Hunter before..." Ally said as she readied the probe.

Kate shook her head and dialed up the radio link to Earth.

* * * * *

Hunter threw the headphones down. "I knew it!" he roared to the room full of hushed mission controllers. "Send a bunch of girls out and what do they do? They drive into a tree, get themselves dragged off by animals for all we know, then expect us to bail them out! Well, it's not going to happen. I told Congress this was a bad idea. Phillips!"

The mission commander appeared at his left side. "I want options! I want to know how much trouble they are in and just what we can tell the press about it. And speaking of the press, where's that PR flack? Hepler!"

Bill Hepler, the press liaison, came up, visibly trembling. He wasn't sure at this moment who he was more afraid of, the irate Hunter or the ravenous mob of journalists just across the hall from the control center. "Sir, the press is anxiously--"

"I don't give a rat's ass about the press. I care about what I'm going to tell the president and those yahoos in Congress! Give me some statement that makes it sound better than it is."

Hepler blanched. "I-I don't know if 'spin' is a good idea right now —"

"Did I ask for your opinion?" His gaze was icy.

"N-no, sir."

"Good, then go write something. And make it snappy!"

Miserably, Hepler slunk away.

"Admiral Hunter?" Another aide stood by, quivering.

Hunter wheeled around, ready to eviscerate whoever dared interrupt him. Before he could spew forth, the aide said quickly, "The president is on the line for you."

It was Hunter's turn to blanch. He nodded at the aide and sat down at his console. Picking up the phone, he put on his most respectful voice. "Good afternoon, Mr. President…"

* * * * *

"Captain, with all due respect, it's not a good idea."

"I know it isn't, No. 1. Unfortunately, they're all lousy ideas right now."

"Someone has to stay aboard. We can't both go down there," Ally said. "Besides, if you go with me, that'll mean I can carry just one person back."

"No, I'd stay. You carry Hanson and the doc back, then return for Smith and me. We'll have a better chance than one alone in getting to the first pod."

Ally had to admit that made sense. "Sir, I have to remind you, if something goes wrong with the pod, there will be no way to get back to the ship. That means there's no way to get the ship home."

"Someone will come along sooner or later, you know that."

That was true. It may take a year or more, but Earth would respond, if for no other reason than to study this amazing planet.

Ally was secretly glad the captain planned to go. She was afraid to go down alone. Still, she was also fearful of abandoning the ship, having no one left to radio messages to her and to be in touch with Earth.

"They'll say we abandoned our posts."

"NASA will have to understand. I want my crew back. I can't go home without them. And I can't send you down alone to fight off their kidnappers."

The bioprobe had confirmed that the away team was in the company of two large humanoids. Considering Greta's injuries, they probably were being carried or were riding through the woods. They appeared to be heading to a pass over the ridge and, ultimately, to the village on the other side, across the plain. Kate was determined to stop them.

Ally nodded. "Aye, aye, sir, I'm convinced. I suppose we need to get NASA's permission, though."

Kate hesitated. She knew her commander was right. She couldn't avoid telling NASA, just because they wanted to solve this themselves. But she was afraid of what Hunter might say.

"OK. I'll call. But we're not waiting any more than two hours for a response. I think we need both of us down there to rescue them and that's what I'm going to recommend to Houston."

Chapter 11

Jorja awoke to find her world had suddenly gotten smaller. She was lying on her back in a wooden cage on a cart, being led through the woods by one of those donkey-like beasts they had seen from the air. The cage was only about four feet high.

Beth's face appeared in her vision. "You all right?"

Jorja couldn't help but notice that the doctor was naked. She tried to sit up and found her hands were tied in front of her. What's more, she was naked too. Beth, though similarly tied, helped her to a sitting position. She looked over to see a nude Greta leaning against the cage wall, her eyes closed, her bound hands resting in her lap. "I'm fine. What-what the hell happened to us?"

"We seem to have become guests of the planet's residents."

"But why are we naked?"

"Apparently, these guys don't like to see women in clothes."

"Jesus. You don't think—"

Beth waited. She could imagine the worries that were flickering through the engineer's mind. She dared not tell her what had happened while both women were unconscious. When the humanoids stripped off Beth's clothes, he appeared to be fascinated with her hairless body. He touched her all over, letting his big hands roam her breasts and cunt. Despite her fear, Beth became aroused.

Lumpy had touched her wetness, then smelled it on his fingers. His large tongue licked them and his eyes widened. He reached down again and Beth had tried to pull away, but the slender native stood right behind her. She felt so small, so helpless sandwiched between these giant-like creatures. She also felt incredibly turned on for some reason. She looked down to see Lumpy's animal skin stretching into a tent.

They spoke to each other in a strange language over her head. Beth felt like an object they were determining the value of. Skinny reached around and touched her heavy breasts. His fingers danced over her nipples, causing her knees to weaken. She could feel his erection as well, poking through his loincloth into her back.

Oddly, instead of being terrified, she sensed that they considered her to be quite a prize and should be handled carefully. She no longer feared for her life—now it was a question of, would they rape her? And if they did, would it be so bad? And they *do* look a lot like humans...she mumbled to herself..

"You don't think they, uh, mate the same way humans do, do you?" Jorja's voice interrupted Beth's thoughts. "That would be an impossible coincidence."

Beth nodded, thinking how close she had come to finding out. "Yes, it would be. Let's hope we're not here long enough to be their guinea pigs in that regard."

"Did they speak to you?"

"Yes, but I can't understand a word. Too bad one of the Utes isn't switched on. It could be gleaning some valuable data."

Beth leaned in and checked the lump on the side of Jorja's face. "How's your head?"

"It's OK. Just a headache. How's the commander?"

Beth shook her head. "Bad headache. The rocking of the cart is making her nauseous."

Greta opened her eyes and tried to smile. "I'm O-OK, Smith." She grimaced and closed her eyes again.

Beth caught Jorja's eye and gave a silent shake of her head. The doctor was clearly worried about the commander.

"Where are they taking us?"

"I don't know, but I'd guess it was the little village we're supposed to be spying on."

"God, NASA's going to skin us alive for this."

"It's not like it's our fault," pointed out Beth.

"It will be by the time Hunter gets through with us. Do we have a weapon? A radio?"

"Nothing. Lumpy here," she indicated the giant driving the cart, "took whatever he could carry—including the Utes, the phasers and my medical kit. We have nothing but the clothes on our—well, never mind."

Jorja knew Beth's attempt at black humor was aimed at keeping their morale up. It wasn't working. Fear gripped her like a physical presence. She also had to pee. Jorja didn't want to relieve herself in front of her peers, even if they were naked.

She looked around. The man Beth called Lumpy rode up front, his broad, hairy back to them. The tall, slender man walked behind, keeping a steady eye on their prizes. "So if that one's Lumpy, what do we call the other man? Skinny?"

Beth gave a short laugh. "Sure, he can be your date."

They fell silent. They were rising slowly into the mountainside on a narrow, switchback trail that was well hidden in the forest.

"So what do you think the captain and the commander will do about this?"

Beth held up her arm and nodded her chin toward the transponder. "They know where we are. And I'm hoping they know we're not wandering off on our own accord. So right now, I'd guess they're trying to decide just how much they can violate the Prime Directive and live with themselves."

"I know what I'd do if the situation was reversed."

"Really? What?"

"I'd come in here like the wrath of god and zap anyone who got in my way. Round up the hostages and blast our way out."

"Don't forget there's only room for two on the pod—if the commander comes alone, as expected. Whoever stays behind could get captured all over again."

"Hell, just give me a couple of fully charged phasers and I'll hold them off for hours. Piece of cake." She did not feel as confident as her words indicated.

"NASA may not let them, you know."

"NASA is a hell of a long way away."

"Well, if they're coming, I'd bet they'll strike before we reach the village."

Jorja nodded. They lapsed into silence again, thinking about what awaited them. Jorja could no longer ignore her bladder. "Shit."

"What's wrong?"

"I have to pee. And I don't think these guys are going to allow a rest stop."

Beth shook her head. "No need. There's a hole at the end of the cart. You can go through there."

Sure enough, Jorja spotted an oval cut out of the floor where the cage overhung the end of the cart. Embarrassed, she slunk down to the end. She had a choice — face Skinny, the leering giant walking behind the cart, or turn and face her peers. Narrowing her eyes, Jorja pretended her piss was acid and sprayed it toward the man behind. He laughed at her as she debased herself, legs spread wide, hanging onto the bars with bound hands, and peed.

For a big woman, Jorja never felt so small.

Chapter 12

The pod was packed and ready to go. Ally and the captain had two phasers to bring along, fully charged. While waiting for NASA's reply, the officers had mapped out their strategy. Once the kidnappers and the away team came down from the mountain ridge, they had to cross a level plain on their way to the village.

They planned to land on the plain, close enough to scare the bejesus out of the humanoids, then both she and the captain would jump out, stunning anyone who dared try to stop them. Free the crew, get Greta and the doc into the bobsled, leaving the captain and Jorja behind with the C4 and the blasting caps.

After the pod left, the two astronauts would pack up any gear that had been left behind, sneak back up the mountain ridge and return to the damaged shuttle. They'd fill the pod with enough C4 to blow it into little pieces— they couldn't leave it to be discovered later. Then they'd walk out onto the dry riverbed and wait.

When Ally returned for them, they'd blow the pod and fly back to the ship. Simple, yet elegant. Now, if only NASA would approve the plan.

The incoming signal light flashed. "Here we go," Kate said.

Hunter got right to the point. "We've reviewed your plan and reluctantly agree that a well-executed rescue mission is preferable to leaving Americans behind on the planet to influence the native population. It is unfortunate that your away team has already violated the Prime Directive. Perhaps a more experienced crew could have avoided the humanoids." Kate seethed.

"However, under no circumstances can Captain Dyson leave the *Letanya*," he intoned from two-million light years away. "That ship represents billions of taxpayers' dollars and you're not going to leave it up there alone for some salvage crew to come along."

What salvage crew this might be in the middle of the Andromeda Galaxy, he didn't say.

"This order comes from the highest level," he continued. To Kate, that meant he came up with it himself. "Commander Egerton is to go down alone and attempt a rescue. Captain Dyson will monitor the operation from orbit. Lt. Commander Smith will return to the damaged shuttle alone to destroy it and await pickup. Report as soon as you have successfully completed your mission. Over and out."

Kate sank back into her seat. *Dammit! I knew I should've just gone ahead!* For a moment, she thought she should go anyway and to hell with Hunter. Her training convinced her otherwise. To violate a direct order would be career suicide. She had invested too much of her life in the space agency to do that. Yet sending Ally down alone was frighteningly risky.

Shit!

"OK, suit up. Looks like we have our marching orders. You're going alone."

Kate thought the commander looked a little stricken when she heard the captain wouldn't be coming along.

Standing by the pod ten minutes later, Ally realized she would not be able to wear the spacesuit. "I can't jump out and fire weapons with a helmet obscuring my vision. Not to mention that I'd have to take my gloves off first."

The captain didn't like it until Ally pointed out that Greta and the doc also would be without suits for the return trip. Because of the tight quarters on the *Letanya*, there was only one spacesuit per person, plus one spare, and the away team's suits were probably left behind at the other shuttle site.

Kate had a better idea. She ordered Ally to stow her suit aboard, plus the captain's and the spare. Once the humanoids were overpowered, three of them could dress for the return trip. If the canopy had been cracked on landing, at least the three would be able to survive the trip back. Ally nodded. It made sense. "You'll be OK up here without a suit?"

"I'm not going anywhere."

In twenty minutes, Ally was ready, strapped into the pod and awaiting the captain's signal. "*Letanya* to Eagle Two, can you read me?"

"Loud and clear, sir."

Kate checked to make sure Ally's subcutaneous transponder was operating normally, then released the pod. "Good luck, commander."

"Roger, captain."

A short time later, Ally dropped through the atmosphere and extended the wings, then checked her heads-up display for the landing site. Three yellow dots blinked at the edge of the plain. Good, they were clear of the trees. She was going to catch the humanoids flatfooted.

"*Letanya*, this is Eagle Two. Have sighted the party. Am going in."

"Roger, Eagle Two. Good luck," Kate said, letting her fingers cross again.

Ally guided the pod in, taking aim at the yellow dots, then sliding to the left just before she touched down. Ally wanted to be close enough to see the expressions on the faces of the natives—and close enough to stun them as soon as she cleared the pod.

Chapter 13

"My god! Look!" Beth pointed at the pod racing in, bouncing to a landing ahead of them. Jorja cheered. Greta just opened her eyes and smiled weakly. Skinny shouted something to Lumpy. The man jumped from the cart and began to pick up stones. Both men rushed toward the pod.

"Shit! They don't seem exactly intimidated," Beth said.

"Come on! They stand no chance against a phaser!"

The landing was near perfect. The pod slid about a hundred yards past the startled group. As soon as it stopped, Ally hit the release button and began unbuckling herself. She heard footfalls and was shocked to see the humanoids rushing the ship. She grabbed two phasers. *Dammit! They aren't supposed to do that! They're supposed to be terrified!*

Ally jumped out and fought panic as she brought the phasers to bear on the huge running men. She fired both at once and was shocked to see them stagger for just a moment before rushing on again. Frantically, she dropped one phaser and twisted the control knob from "1" to "2" on the other, then raised it to fire at the leading man.

The blast caught him in the chest and he took one step and fell heavily into the sand. Ally swung the gun around just as something flicked into her field of vision. She felt a sudden pain in her forehead. She pulled the trigger just as she blacked out.

Ally awoke to gentle rocking motion. For a moment, she thought she was back aboard the pod, being buffeted by upper atmospheric winds. *Did I rescue them?* She opened her eyes fully to see quite a different scene. She was wedged in the back of the caged cart with the other three women. All were looking at her with concern mixed with disappointment.

They were also all naked. That shocked her until she realized she was naked too. Her hands were tied in front of her.

"Are you all right?" Beth leaned over to touch her head with similarly bound hands. Ally winced.

"What the hell happened?"

"These guys are pretty good at throwing rocks," the doctor explained. "One of them hit you before you could drop him."

Beth decided not to tell her how Lumpy and Skinny stripped the unconscious woman of her clothes, talking giddily to each other when they discovered she was the same as their other captives. The three astronauts watched silently as the giants fondled Ally's breasts and pussy, paying particular attention to her lack of hair. For reasons they didn't understand, they didn't rape her while she was out. They simply loaded her into the cart with the others and rode on.

"The stun setting didn't stop them," Ally muttered. The enormity of what happened hit her and she began to cry. "I was the captain's only hope," she sobbed. "Dyson wanted to come with me, but Hunter overruled her. We could've taken them easy with two of us!"

Briefly, Ally explained the plans they had drawn up and NASA's orders.

"We're not dead yet," Jorja said. "They didn't touch the pod—it seemed to scare them, and not much scares these guys. If we can get away, three of you can fly out of here." She didn't say what she was thinking—that the pod might soon be swarmed with villagers, all curious about the alien bird.

"But now they have all our weapons! We're helpless without them." She sat up. "Shit! Why did they take our clothes? They can't possibly be interested in us. I mean, would you want to have sex with an alien?"

"We've been talking about that," Beth said gently. "Best we can figure it, they've mistaken us for the women of their own planet."

"But we don't look like them!"

"Actually, we do. Yes, they have that ridge on their foreheads and more body hair, but otherwise, they appear to be a sister race."

"How could that be? Two races two-million light years apart?"

Jorja shrugged. "Score one for the creationists," she said, her voice laced with sarcasm.

"Don't be so dismissive," Beth replied. "It may be true that there's some controlling authority over the universe. How else can you explain it?"

"So you mean, in addition to being stranded, we may become the, uh, property of these men?" Ally was appalled.

"I don't know their customs. That's what we were coming down to find out," Beth said.

"Only now, we're going to get a more up close and personal view," Jorja said.

Chapter 14

Kate hit the radio switch again. "*Letanya* to Eagle Two, *Letanya* to Eagle Two." Static hissed in the speakers. Tears clouded her vision. She called up the transponder signals and saw all four grouped tightly together, well past the pod, moving slowly into the village.

Something had gone horribly wrong and she was helpless to do anything about it. *Damn Hunter!* Kate knew she should've violated orders. *This would not have happened if I had gone with her.*

She closed her eyes for a moment to think about her limited options. The *Letanya* had a space cannon in the event it was attacked by another ship, but it did not have a weapon that could cut through the atmosphere and reach the planet. A cannon shell would simply burn up and explode eighty thousand feet up. It wouldn't matter even if they had such a weapon—if use of a phaser was a violation of the rules, how would NASA react to a request to blast the planet? And how would that save the crew anyway?

She could wait until another ship could be sent. That would take approximately a year. To survive a year up here, she'd have to go back into cryosleep and abandon the women to their fates below. No way.

Kate had to report in. Maybe NASA has some ideas. *Damn! This is just what Hunter had warned about!* She had no choice. The captain dialed up the radio transmitter, knowing her career was over at this moment. Only history would tell if she would be branded an idiot or a coward. Some choice.

"Houston, this is the *U.S.S. Letanya*. My worst fears have been realized. Following orders instead of acting on my instincts, I sent Commander Egerton down alone to rescue the members of the away team. I received a brief message just before landing and everything appeared normal. However, it was the last I heard from her. Now, according to the transponders, all four women are being taken together into the village. I'm stuck up here without a pod—"

Suddenly she stopped, eyes wide. *The escape pods!*

She narrowed her eyes and looked directly into the camera as if it was Hunter's face. "No, that's not true, is it, Hunter? I've got an escape pod." Kate hit the pause switch, thinking rapidly. A plan formulated in her mind. She hit 'Resume.' "Here's what I'm going to do, Hunter, uh, Houston, and by the time you receive this, it will already have been done, so ordering me not to will have no effect. I'm going to take the escape pod down to the surface, go in and rescue my crew. If we can, we'll return to the shuttle pod, providing it's undamaged, and send Commander Egerton, Dr. Reyes and the injured Commander Hanson back to the ship. Lt. Commander Smith and I will proceed to the first pod as originally planned to destroy it. Commander Egerton will return for us after refueling.

"I fully realize I am violating your orders. I know my career will be over whether I succeed or not. But at least I will have done something to try to save my crew. If I fail, you won't hear from me or my crew again. We don't expect a rescue. We knew the risks when we took on this mission. The only request I make is that you see if you can pick up our transponder signals when another ship arrives. This is Captain Kathryn Dyson of the *U.S.S. Letanya*, out."

She sent the message, and sat back. Pausing just a moment to reflect on the enormity of her undertaking, she re-keyed the signal and started a new message. "Houston, this is *U.S.S. Letanya*, requesting you send this personal message to the families of the crew." Kate already could feel the tears burning her eyes. "Brian and Donnie; Bill, Robert and Margaret..." Kate ran down the list of family members of her crew by memory. "I wanted to take this moment to tell you what happened to the crew and how bravely they performed their duties."

Kate described the pod flights, how everyone was cool under pressure and the brave decision by Commander Egerton to go down alone to attempt a rescue. "I know they all loved you very much. I'm going down now to follow in Allyson's footsteps and try to bring them all back home to you. I know they would do the same for me or any other crew member. Wish me luck. Captain Dyson, out."

Kate put the ship into automatic mode, which should keep it in orbit until someone could come along and claim it if she was unable to return. She stopped by sick bay and injected herself with a transponder. She doubted the signal would last a year, but it was the only way a rescue ship could find her. Hell, in a year, they'd probably all be dead anyway.

Kate pulled the last phaser out of its holder and checked to make sure it was fully charged. She moved to the escape pod. There were two pods aboard the shuttle. Each could hold up to three persons, although it would be a tight fit. They were designed for one-way transport down to a planet, or between ships. They had no engine and limited thruster control. A computer aimed the pod at the right angle to bore through the atmosphere, then the chute deployed, carrying the pod to the surface.

To try and aim the pod at the landing site of the second pod would be like trying to score a hole-in-one on a par four. The best Kate could hope for was to land somewhere within a few miles of the site. Even that would be miraculous, considering she'd be flying the aerodynamic equivalent of a stone.

She went to the bridge to check the latest photos.

Chapter 15

"We've got to get them to turn on the U.T.s," Ally said. "If we can communicate with them, we might be able to convince them to let us go."

"I don't understand why they weren't more scared of us," Jorja said, shifting her position to relieve her aching muscles. "I mean, picture how we'd react if an alien ship landed in Central Park. There'd be screaming in the streets!"

"They don't seem to be an excitable bunch, that's for sure. Maybe they're just *very* confident."

Ally wanted to keep the group focused on escape. "OK, barring talking to them or scaring them to death, how do we get out of here? The pod is just sitting there, waiting for us. If we can get just a little lead on them, we can jump in and take off."

"That won't work—Greta can't run," Beth pointed out.

Ally looked at the commander. Greta was pale. The gash on her head glared red and blue. She opened her eyes upon hearing her name and Ally could tell the light hurt her eyes. That wasn't a good sign.

"All right. We need to get to our weapons," Ally said. "Then we can blast our way out. Anyone know where they have them?"

"I think they're in that bag by Lumpy," Jorja said, pointing.

"Are our clothes in there too?" Ally asked hopefully.

"No," Beth said. "They dropped them by the road."

The bag was about two feet away, but it might as well have been two hundred feet. They couldn't reach it through the wooden bars of the cage and even if they could, the hulking back of the driver loomed right next to it. He'd break anyone's arm that came close.

There was nothing the women could do. The cart rolled on. Soon the village came into view. Their hearts sank. What little chance they had would become smaller once they were surrounded by the villagers.

"I wonder what the captain is doing right now?" Ally asked.

"Probably pulling her hair out. She knows where we are—she just has no way of reaching us," Jorja said.

"I'll bet she's burning up the airwaves between here and Earth," Beth said.

The cart came to the edge of the village. All of the captives except Greta sat up and looked at it with calculating eyes, refusing to give up hope that they'd find a way out. The village was composed of huts, made out of mud bricks, and some crude log cabins. Wide, dusty streets separated the groupings of structures. There were many men, dressed similarly to the ones with them. They strutted like peacocks through the streets. The crew saw women for the first time, walking behind the men, their heads bowed slightly. Many were on leashes! They appeared so small compared to the giants. They were also universally naked.

Villagers paid the captives no attention at first— perhaps they were thought to be just another prisoner transport. Then a man noticed their lack of body hair and lighter complexions and pointed, talking in that melodious language to a companion. Soon others noticed and began to approach the cart. Beth, the anthropologist of the group, observed that the women didn't take any action on their own, they merely followed the men, even if they weren't leashed.

Off to the side, near a log building, Beth caught sight of a couple. She stared, unable to believe her eyes. The man was signaling to the woman. She was naked and had wispy hair between her breasts and thicker hair in her armpits, on her pubis, legs and arms. Without hesitation, she braced herself against the building, her head low. The man pulled his loincloth aside and let his erection come free. It was large, but otherwise looked human. Beth couldn't fathom how the sex organs of these humanoids could be nearly identical to the men of Earth. She also was stunned that she was about to see a couple mate right out here on the street.

Sure enough, the man pressed himself against her from behind and his cock disappeared from view. The woman braced herself as the man began pumping—the same way a man of Earth would, Beth noted. She observed the woman reach down between her legs and rub herself, indicating the women probably had clitorises on this planet, just like the women of Earth.

The cart rolled on before Beth could see any more. She sat back, stunned by the meaning of her observation. The shockwaves would be felt all the way to Earth. If two species separated by such a great distance could be so similar, what did that say about the very fabric of the universe? The vast universe would be a lot more cohesive and organized than anyone previously had thought.

A small crowd gathered as the cart approached the main square. Skinny, walking behind, began answering their questions, waving his arms, his voice rising and falling. Murmurs filtered through the crowd as the man's words were relayed to newcomers. By the time the cart stopped near a large platform, the crowd had grown to more than fifty. The driver reined in the donkey, then stood. The crowd seemed to fall back slightly. Beth thought Lumpy must be an important figure to the villagers.

He came around to the back and unlocked the cage. There was no chance for the crew to try to overpower him, not with the crowd behind, so they allowed themselves to be taken out, one by one, and let him tie their hands behind them. They were led up the stairs to the platform. Greta limped and staggered, unable to maintain her balance. The man's partner held her up easily with a large hand wrapped around her upper arm.

The women were embarrassed to be naked in front of the crowd, regardless that it may be the custom for the women of this world. They were directed to stand before thick wooden posts and their hands were untied, then retied around them. They could barely move. They hung their heads in shame.

Lumpy walked the platform, speaking to the crowd, gesturing to the captives. The crowd appeared to be impressed by them. He said something and the crowd reacted, almost derisively, Beth thought. The man's face darkened and he said something to his partner. Skinny approached Ally and untied her, bringing her forward.

When she stood next to Lumpy, he said something to her and pointed at the crowd. Ally, embarrassed at being put on display, didn't understand what he was trying to say. He gestured again, growing angry. Ally just shook her head, tears falling from her eyes. Her heart pounded. She wished she could understand him.

He grabbed her jaw and waggled it. Oh! He wanted her to speak, to show they weren't from around here, she realized. Duh. That should already be obvious. "My name is Allyson Egerton," she said in a firm voice. "I am commander of a space ship. We come from Earth. We mean you no harm, but we would like to be released so that we may return to our ship."

Her words electrified the audience. They stared, open-mouthed, then began talking anew amongst themselves.

Ally knew they couldn't understand her, but it made her feel better to stand up and speak for the people of Earth. She turned to Lumpy. "If you would get our translators out of the bag, we could begin to talk to each other." The man just stared at her. Ally pointed as best she could with her hands behind her back toward the cart parked below. "The bag, you big galoot, the bag."

The man cocked his head, then said something to Skinny. Ally was relieved to see the man return to the cart and retrieve the bag. These beings were highly intelligent! He returned to hand the bag to his partner. Lumpy began pawing through it. He pulled out a phaser and held it up to the crowd. There was more murmuring. He held it clumsily, finally fitting his fingers around the grip. The gun was small in his hands. By luck, his finger touched the trigger, but, of course, he was locked out. To him, the object would be useless. He dropped the gun into the bag and pulled out a U.T.

"Yes!" Ally shouted. Behind her, Beth and Jorja shouted as well. Curious, the man held it closer to his face, trying to understand its significance. "Turn the switch on the side," she said, desperate for him to understand. "It's going to take awhile to work, but let's get started, OK?"

He wasn't getting it. Frustrated, Ally indicated to the partner that he could cut her ropes. She gestured again and again. Words were exchanged between the two men. The big man shook his head. He didn't trust the pilot who blasted him twice.

Ally watched as the man slipped the Ute into a pouch hanging from his belt. Her heart fell as she was dragged back to the post and retied. "Noooo! Listen to me! We can talk to each other!"

The partner pinched Ally's nipple, hard, and she squealed, then shut up. She didn't say anything when he reached down and stroked her bare pussy. Ally was beyond embarrassment at this point. The other captives watched dejectedly. Greta just hung from her bindings, her eyes closed.

The big man again spoke to the crowd. Some responded excitedly.

"You know what's happening, don't you?" Beth said to Ally, who was fastened to the adjacent post.

"I think so, but I'm afraid to believe it."

"I'm afraid it's true. We're being auctioned off."

"How could they? Would we do that to E.T.?"

"They don't think of us as alien—just as foreigners, like we came from another continent. We probably look exotic to them, like Swedes might look to the Spanish or vise versa. You know, this culture is not all that dissimilar from ours, once upon a time."

Ally looked over at the anthropologist. "This isn't helping, doc. I want to hear how we're going to tell them otherwise, without the Ute."

Beth looked back at the big man talking up the crowd. "Maybe we'll have to learn their language the old-fashioned way."

Chapter 16

Kate studied the latest photos with a magnifying glass. She wanted to memorize the layout of the town, especially the town square. When the most recent photo fell out of the digital processor, she turned white with fear — and fury — as she held it up to the light. Unless she was mistaken, her four crew women were all being held on some sort of platform, bound to stakes. They appeared to be naked, just like all the other women in town.

"Dammit, Ally, how could you let them take you?" Kate knew she was missing something. Somehow these sixteenth century beings managed to overpower an intelligent, alert woman armed with a late-21st century weapon. What had happened?

She would have to be very careful.

Taking one last look, she climbed down the ladder into the escape pod. Kate paused before she slipped inside, looking around her ship. It may be the last time she would see it. But she had no choice. She was going to rescue her crew or die trying.

Kate glanced at her chronometer as she strapped herself in. Nearly an hour and a half had passed since she radioed Earth. It had taken some time to reposition the ship to give her the best aim at landing near the second pod. The pod would travel nearly all the way around the planet as it made its way through the atmosphere. Once it was in the upper atmosphere, she'd have to hope that her calculations about the prevailing winds were accurate.

Otherwise, she might end up two hundred kilometers away.

She decided to launch before guilt made her wait for NASA's response. She had no doubt that Hunter would be sending one, probably to tell her "under no circumstances" should she leave the ship. Screw him. She bolted the door and fastened her restraints.

"Hey, it was a nice career," she said out loud and pulled the launch handle.

The escape pod was designed to rocket away from the bay door, in the event the ship was about to explode. She hung on grimly as the G-forces pressed her back in her seat. Kate let the computer aim the pod at the right angle to pierce the atmosphere.

Within minutes, she felt the craft being buffeted. Red streaks and sparks flew past the two oval windows. Her heart pounded and she wasn't sure if the bumpy ride was responsible, or her overwhelming knowledge that she was the crew's last hope.

Kate read the instruments, using her training to calm her down. When she hit ninety thousand feet, the heat began to dissipate. At eighty thousand, blue skies returned to the two portholes. She waited several long seconds, then saw the panel flash green. She held on until her position matched the best guess of the computer. She pulled a lever. A moment later, she felt the reassuring lift from the parachute. Leaning down, she could look up through one of the portholes to see it open above the pod.

Thank god! That's one worry gone. Now if I can just land close!

The winds were strong. Kate watched the screen that showed the blips from where the second pod had landed and where the crew was being held. They were still in the village, grouped together near the center. Kate watched, dismayed, as the winds carried her rapidly toward the second pod. She glanced at the altimeter: forty thousand feet. Dammit! She was going to overshoot it by several kilometers. She began firing the forward thrusters to slow down her rate of drift.

The second pod slipped by underneath as she passed eighteen thousand feet. A mountain ridge appeared in her windows. She calculated her rate of descent and the approaching mountain and thought she just might get down before she was dashed to death on its cliff face. "Come on! Come on!" Kate fired the thrusters again. The pod rocked, then leaped forward again. She couldn't fight the wind for long.

The ridge filled the windows as she came down the last five thousand feet. She had saved a little fuel and used it just before landing, cutting the chute loose at the same time to avoid being dragged. The pod bumped down underneath the brow of the angry butte.

Kate popped the hatch and crawled out. She checked her portable scanner and found she was thirty-six kilometers from the pod, and thirty-eight klicks from the village. Actually not too bad, considering. She took her supplies, including her phaser and a Ute. If talking didn't work, she carried a few cubes of explosives and blasting caps. Bet they haven't invented C4, she thought.

She wrapped the remaining explosives around a detonator and set the timer for thirty minutes. That should give her plenty of time to get away. She dropped the bundle into the pod and shut the hatch. "Sorry to do this to you, old friend, but I can't leave you here for the natives to discover," she said.

Then, without a backward glance, she turned and headed for the village.

Chapter 17

Jorja stood before the crowd, trying to ignore the leering and shouts. She had been dragged to the front and displayed like so much horseflesh, made to walk back and forth while one of the men held her firmly by her upper arm. Jorja was a big woman, but she was petite compared to these men.

Lumpy touched Jorja's breasts and cunt, displaying their uniqueness to the crowd. Like a used car salesmen, she imagined him saying, "Low mileage! Smooth styling! Still under warranty!"

Beth watched from her post, fascinated, despite her fear. The anthropologist in her found the actions displayed by these humanoids paralleled Earth's own history. Throughout time, the selling of slaves was commonplace. It was inconceivable now to imagine, but back then, humans of one ethnicity often felt morally superior to those of a different ethnic background. The Pharaohs enslaved the Jews, the Spaniards overwhelmed the Incas, heck, even the Americans brought Africans over to work their cotton plantations. What made this culture different is that they apparently enslaved an entire gender.

She had seen the way women behaved here, just in the few minutes they had been in town. While it was difficult to tell from the ship, at ground level it was obvious women were docile and obedient. They followed behind their men, awaiting directions, even if they weren't leashed. It was not unlike some Mideastern countries of Earth, only those women were always covered up. Here, nakedness simply accentuated their subjugation. It certainly made them more accessible for sex, she noted.

Beth attributed much of the cultural development to the imposing physical differences between the sexes. On Earth, the women were not all that much smaller and some women were even larger than the men. On Devon, all of the men she had seen so far were well over six feet, while the women were usually under five-eight, although it was hard to tell because many walked with their heads bowed.

This planet represented a monumental discovery that the doctor would enjoy exploring for years — but not as a participant, she reflected, pulling at her bonds. It's one thing to observe how the Romans treated the Christians, it's quite another to be thrown into the lion's pit with the underdogs.

Beth heard the man repeat one word often to the crowd that sounded like, *"detashia."* In context, she wondered if that meant "fair-skinned" or "exotic" or "valuable." Maybe it just meant "hairless." She was determined to learn their language, rather than wait for the Utes.

Jorja brought a number of bids before one man apparently won. There was some exciting jabbering, then the man came forward, trailed by a younger man and a woman. The man was even taller than Lumpy, Beth noticed. He had gray hair and a beard and seemed to command a certain amount of respect.

She thought the younger man might be his son. He had the same eyes set in a thin sallow face. If he had been an Earthman, she'd guess his age would be about twenty. The woman behind him seemed older, but Beth wasn't sure if the woman was his mother, a slave — or both. In fact, the whole family dynamic would make a fascinating study.

Jorja struggled. She did not want to be separated from her crew members. She shouted at the men, angry and afraid. The buyer just laughed. He seemed amused by the spirited woman. He may live to regret that, Beth thought. She knew that Jorja was a black belt in karate and had taught classes for years, even while serving as an astronaut.

Money — or what seemed to be money — exchanged hands and the buyer roughly grabbed Jorja off the platform and pushed her at the younger man. He smiled and bent over to look at her lack of hair between her legs, jabbering comments. Jorja cursed at him. The young man picked her up as if she was a child and slung her over his shoulder. He strode away through the crowd. The older man stood there with his wife/slave and watched, puffing his chest with pride.

Beth was taken up next to be auctioned. Because she stood just five-four, there was no way she was going to resist like Jorja did. Lumpy could break her spine if he chose to. She allowed herself to be walked back and forth. She gritted her teeth when his fingers probed her breasts and privates. It wasn't at all arousing this time.

The bids weren't as numerous as Jorja's had been, which hurt Beth's feelings. *If they knew I was a doctor, I'll bet they'd bid higher.* She caught herself, surprised she would think such degrading thoughts. Beth hadn't heard that word, *detashia,* and thought about the differences between her and Jorja. Perhaps it simply meant "big."

An older man in the crowd won the bid and came up to claim her. Beth looked him over carefully, wondering what she should expect from the humanoid. He looked harmless enough. Standing about six-three, he was actually one of the shortest men in the crowd. Beth wondered how long these natives lived, what they ate, what type of educational system they had. *So many questions!* She hoped she would be well treated while she tried to discover the answers to them.

When Beth was brought down from the platform, she got a close look at her new captor. The man had a kindly face, reasonably clean-shaven. Close up, she could tell he was middle-aged—there was some gray in his spiky hair. For that reason, she thought of him as "Spike." Beth couldn't imagine she'd have much trouble from him, even if he did try and mate with her. After all, how many times could he get it up? Of course, she realized she was comparing him to an Earth man. Here, they might get hard-ons well into their eighties!

He fastened a collar around her neck and attached a leash to it. She expected to be taken away immediately, and was glad to see him stick around for the rest of the auction. She was really worried about Greta. As he stood next to her, he began idly stroking her breasts and smiling. Apparently, he liked the smooth skin on these new slaves.

Ally was brought up next and quickly sold to a man who already had three women in tow. She couldn't imagine why he'd need another woman in his life. The man was close to seven feet tall, which made Ally look like a child next to him. He hardly paid any attention to her, letting his women leash her and drag her along behind them as he walked away.

Beth, watching and listening closely, again heard that word *detashia* used. Ally wasn't much taller than Beth, so it couldn't be "big." *Spirited*, perhaps? *Pretty? Valuable?*

Greta came up last. Beth saw that she was still quite dizzy and had trouble standing up on her own. Her captors treated her like damaged goods and the crowd reacted accordingly. Very few bids were offered. The two men seemed upset over their captive. They shouted at her to straighten up and walk. Her injuries prevented her from doing what they wanted. Beth was very worried about her. Surely they can see the wound on her head—don't they have any medical help on this godforsaken planet?

"*Detashia*," she said suddenly to her new owner, pointing to Greta. He looked surprised.

"*Detashia?*" he repeated, quizzically, looking up at the limping woman.

Beth grabbed his hand and stroked her skin with it, mimicking his actions of a few minutes before. "Yes, she's valuable merchandise," she said in exasperation. "Buy her, you old goat—I know you like the smooth ones. Besides, I can help her."

Spike looked around, as if thinking about what she had said. Beth held her breath, wishing she knew exactly what the word meant. She hoped it meant "valuable."

"*Qwitan*," the man said suddenly, raising his hand.

Lumpy looked down at him. "*Qwitan?*"

The man nodded. Lumpy looked out over the crowd and said a few more words. There was silence. He looked back to the man and nodded, scowling. He brought Greta to the edge of the platform.

"Let me help her," Beth said, holding up her bound hands, tipping her head toward Greta. Spike looked at her for a moment, then took out a knife and cut her free. She wasn't going anywhere, not with the leash on her. Beth turned to Greta and with the man's help, brought her down to the ground. The commander sagged in her arms.

"It's all right, commander, I've got you. You get to go with me. You're going to be fine." Beth wished she could be sure of that.

Beth braced herself against the weight of the larger woman. Their buyer made no effort to help. It's probably a cultural thing, she mused. Owners don't help slaves. But when they reached the man's cart, parked at the edge of the square, he helped Beth lift Greta into the back. He put a collar and leash on Greta and tied both leashes to the cart. Then he clucked his tongue at the donkey and the two astronauts rode off toward their new lives.

Chapter 18

Jorja, collared and leashed, was dragged along by the young man toward their cart. The older man and his slave followed behind.

The younger man gave her orders that she didn't understand and began to get angry until the old man caught up and spoke a few words to his son. The older man turned and gave the same orders to the woman with them and she immediately braced herself against the cart, head low. The older man stepped up behind her and pulled his loincloth aside.

Jorja turned to the young man. "Oh, no! Not that! I'm from another planet! I don't belong here! We aren't even the same species!" She was desperate not to let this happen. She imagined fatal consequences from such an intimate liaison.

The boy was not to be denied. He grabbed her and forced her head down next to the slave woman. Jorja tried to struggle. On Earth, she would have been able to fight off most men. Here, the men were more than a match for her. Still, she had to do *something*.

Instinctively, she brought up her right leg and kicked back, catching him in the groin. He doubled over and Jorja turned and brought her knee up into his face, hearing the satisfying crunch of cartilage. The old man just stared at her, his cock pinning the slave girl to the cart.

Enraged, the young man tried to backhand Jorja across the face, but she blocked it and punched him hard

in the stomach. He stepped back, gasping and she
followed with a front kick that sent him sprawling onto the
ground.

He jumped up, enraged, looking around wildly to see
if anyone had seen him getting beaten up by a woman.
There were several people standing around, staring. He
charged the Earth woman angrily, ready to use his
superior weight and strength to knock her down. Instead,
she sidestepped and tripped him, using his momentum
against him. He fell headfirst into the dirt again. He cried
out in fury and frustration and began to scramble to his
feet.

She froze there for a moment as the full weight of her
rash actions hit her. Jorja sensed that on this planet, no
woman would probably ever dare to do what she had
done. No doubt there would be severe repercussions. In an
instant, her fear galvanized her into action. She turned and
ran down the main street, her leash flapping behind her.

Jorja heard the old man shouting. She didn't look
back. Several men came out to stare at her as she sprinted
past, as if they couldn't believe their eyes. Then, at first just
one or two and then in larger numbers, they began to
intervene. Reaching out for her, they tried to grab her
arms. One dove for her legs, but she managed to jump
over his back.

Her breath was coming in gasps in the hot
atmosphere. The natives were used to it and they came at
her from all directions now. She fought them, using knees,
elbows and speed. She kicked, she punched, she used all
her skills. Still, there were just too many. Someone
managed to trip her and she fell heavily into the dirty
street. She cried out as three big men pinned her to the
ground.

The crowd parted as her new "owners" approached. Jorja could see blood on the face of the younger man. He was clearly furious. The older man tried to talk to him, but the younger man just shrugged him off. *Uh oh, I'm in trouble now*, she thought. She struggled again. The men held her firmly.

The young man unhooked the leash and doubled it. He slashed out suddenly, catching her on the legs, the leather stinging her flesh. Jorja cried out.

"*Junga!*" A tall, elderly man stepped between Jorja and the angry young man. Instantly, the crowd went silent and stepped back. Clearly, this man commanded respect. Perhaps he was a village leader, she mused. He said a few sentences to the father. The young man didn't like what he heard, but his father smiled. He nodded his head in agreement.

The son stepped forward, gesticulating wildly. The town elder listened, then spoke a few words. The young man cocked his head, then looked at Jorja. His father took him aside and whispered something into his ear. Slowly, the son nodded and gave a grim, bloody smile.

"*Solume jamkalut,*" he said to the elder.

The crowd cheered suddenly, startling Jorja. Her arms were held behind her back while leather straps were fastened. Two men bent down and hobbled her ankles. *What the hell is going on?*

Chapter 19

Beth, supporting Greta, groaned under the larger woman's weight. They had arrived at Spike's house and she was left to get Greta inside. There was no chance of escaping—she might be able to get away, but she'd have to leave the mission commander behind. The humanoid seemed to know she would never do that.

Beth eased the woman through the door. The man gestured to indicate a crude couch where Greta should be placed. He moved closer, indicating some disgust with his purchase. He said something that Beth took to mean he was sorry he let her talk him into it.

"I can help her," she said, knowing he wouldn't understand. She pointed at Greta's wound, then to herself.

The man looked at her quizzically. "If I could get my medical kit from Lumpy, I could help her get better." Beth held up her hands and showed the size of the case. "The auctioneer has it," she said, trying out her meager charades to recreate the auction. He cocked his head.

"*Ambrusta?*"

"Well, if that is the man's name, then, yes. Or maybe that's what you call an auction here, huh?" Beth was frustrated. "Dammit! My kingdom for a Ute!"

Maybe that was the answer! She held up her hands again, only this time, sizing a much smaller object. "*Ambrusta* held it up, remember? If I can get one, we can talk." She moved her hand between her mouth and his.

"*Gorshun?*" The man nodded. He took a fine chain out of a nearby cabinet, then reached down and fastened one end to the collar around Greta's neck. He locked the other to a metal ring at one end of the couch.

"*Gorshun dingat toruka,*" he said and headed for the door, tugging on her leash.

"Yes!" Maybe she was getting through to him. She followed Spike back to the cart and started to climb into the front. He looked at her, aghast, and she realized a slave was not supposed to act this way. Reluctantly, she let him lead her to the back where he tied her into place like a dog.

Clucking at the donkey-beast, the man snapped the reins. The cart jerked forward. In minutes, they passed the main square, then turned down a side street. The man stopped near a nondescript hut. Untying her, he led her inside without knocking. Beth recognized Lumpy immediately. A slave woman was in one corner, cooking something over a small fire that was vented by a hole in the ceiling.

"What do you do if it rains," she wondered aloud. No one paid her any attention.

The slave trader and Spike talked for a few minutes. Beth listened carefully, trying to pick up some words. The man said the word "*rushnak*" a couple of times when he was indicating the size of the device that Beth had referred to.

The trader went to this pouch and pulled out the Ute. "Yes!" Beth said loudly, startling both men. She pointed at it. "*Rushnak.*" She hoped she was using the word correctly. She reached out for it. *Just let me have it long enough to turn it on!*

Lumpy shook his head. He spoke to the man, then pulled one of the phase pistols from his bag. He pointed, indicating something coming out of the end, then slapped his chest and said a few words, including what sounded like "*Darmsek.*" Did that mean pain? Or danger?

Beth shook her head and pointed to it again. "Just turn the switch on the side, you dolts!" She tried to show it to them. Spike and Lumpy huddled together, turning the Ute over and over, trying to understand its mysteries. By accident, Lumpy hit the switch that caused a red light to glow on it. They pulled away. Lumpy held it at arm's length.

"Yes, that's it," Beth tried to keep the excitement out of her voice, so she wouldn't startle the big men. "That's all there is to it. Now just speak normally. It will take about an hour before we have a minimal translation. When the light turns to yellow, that's when you'll know. And when it switches to green, we can talk normally with it." Beth knew they didn't understand a word.

There was more discussion between the two men. Spike wanted to take it with him, but Lumpy was reluctant to part with it. Some money exchanged hands and Lumpy handed it over.

"Now, what about my medical kit?" Beth was pushing her luck. She again showed the size of the kit.

The man's brow furrowed. He spoke a few words to Lumpy. The slave trader shook his head. More words were exchanged. Beth held her breath. Lumpy dug through his bag and found the case. He held it up.

"Yes, that's it," Beth said quietly. She looked at Spike and pantomimed the cut on Greta's forehead. "Please. I could use it to help my friend. And your valuable property." She didn't believe that, but she hoped her tone might convey her concern.

Lumpy opened the kit and examined the bottles, syringes, pills and bandages within. He looked up at the man and apparently named his price. Spike laughed and shook his head. They went back and forth. Clearly, Lumpy wanted too much for it.

"Wait." Beth stepped forward, pantomiming being allowed to touch it. Lumpy pushed her away. She turned to the man, and pointed to her forehead again, making a small slashing move with her finger, then held up her thumb and forefinger, an inch apart. "I just need a little something to help Greta's wound."

Spike spoke again. Lumpy went to a table and picked up a crudely sharpened knife. He returned, then nodded slowly at Beth. His meaning was clear — don't try anything funny. Beth sidled closer to the kit, keeping her eyes on Lumpy, trying to act submissive.

He allowed her to select some bandaging, adhesive tape, alcohol and a few headache tablets. When she tried to take a syringe and a sedative, he balked and waved the knife threateningly at her. She retreated. She opened her hands to show the meager items she had taken.

More words were exchanged. Spike gave him a few more coins. Lumpy was getting angry, so it was time for a quick retreat. In minutes, they were back in the cart, heading for home. The man held the Ute. Beth gripped the medicines to her chest and prayed that Greta would be able to recover from the concussion mostly on her own.

Greta hadn't moved while they were gone. "Hi, Greta. I've got something for that gash on your head." She bent down, examining the wound on her forehead. She wished she had a needle and thread. Greta would end up with a nasty little scar.

She turned to Spike. "Water? Do you have some water?"

The man stared at her. Beth looked around and spotted a wooden bucket with a cover on a table near the corner. She strode over to it and lifted the lid. *Aha!* "Water," she said, splashing the liquid with her fingers.

"*Vama*," the man replied.

Beth held out her hand for the Ute. He hesitated, then handed it to her. He was afraid it might be a weapon, she realized. "*Vama*," she said into the machine, then pressed a button on the front. "Water." The machine repeated the words. Spike's eyes widened when it spoke for the first time. He stepped back.

She knew she was scaring the man, but it was important to jump-start the U.T. by giving it equivalencies. She would do many more in the hours to come. She handed the U.T. back to the startled man to show that it was harmless.

Taking a coarsely woven cloth from the tabletop, the doctor dipped half of it into the water, then returned to clean Greta's wound. She put alcohol on a section of the dry cloth and disinfected the area. In a few more minutes, she had a bandage over the wound. Greta seemed to come to. She smiled at the doctor. "Thanks."

The old man just watched her, fascinated. *Don't they have doctors on this planet? What if someone breaks a leg?*

Returning to the water, Beth dipped a cup into it and gave Greta the headache pills, letting her swallow a little water. "I wish I had my scanner. I could see how that concussion is doing," she remarked.

"It's OK. I think I'm feeling a little better," Greta said. "Where are we?"

"This man bought us at the auction, remember?

"Bought us?" Her memory was spotty.

"Yes. I think that means we're his property," she said. "But he seems harmless. Best of all, I convinced him to get us a Ute!"

Greta sat up. "We've got a Ute?"

Beth nodded. "It's processing. With the Spike's help, I hope to accelerate its learning curve."

"Spike?" She giggled, seeing his hair. "God, yes. I'd love to be able to talk to these guys." She grimaced.

"Hey, don't overdo it. You should rest. You might feel better tomorrow."

She nodded and closed her eyes. In minutes, she fell asleep again.

Beth looked around the room and identified several items that would have English equivalents. She motioned the man over. "Table," she said.

"*Lukita.*"

She showed him how to press the button to tell the machine of a direct counterpart. Over the next half-hour, Beth programmed three dozen words. She checked the light on the device—it still glowed red. It needed more time.

"So, tell me about yourself," she told the old man. "Why did you buy us? You don't seem like the slave-owning type."

The man shook his head.

"I know you don't know what I'm saying, just talk to me," she insisted, pointing to the device.

The man spoke a few words, then fell silent. Just like a man, he wasn't much of a talker. Beth got another idea. She approached him. Taking one of his hands into hers, she brought it to her breast. "Breast," she said.

"*Murisk*," he murmured. She pointed to the Ute. He pressed the button and repeated the words. He seemed less afraid of the machine now. That was one big difference between these people and Earthlings of the 16th century, she realized. The Devonites were more willing to adapt to change. A device like this on Earth during that time would've sent most men screaming, only to return later to burn Beth at the stake. Perhaps they didn't have the strong religious influences that they have on Earth.

She touched other body parts, her arm, her head, her leg, getting the humanoid's response in return. Beth was beginning to feel a certain kinship with this man. So she stroked the outside of his loincloth and said, "Penis."

Confusion flitted across his face. He pulled at the loincloth. "*Naronga?*"

Beth slid her hand past the leather thong holding the garment into place and let her hand touch his cock. "Penis," she repeated. It twitched and began to stiffen in her hand. *My god, it's huge,* she thought.

He smiled and looked down. "*Gangar*," he said softly. Beth took the Ute from his unresisting finger and repeated the words. "I'll bet that's not the only word you have for it, huh?"

Spike surprised her when he reached out and cupped his hand over her bare mound, letting his fingers cover her cleft. "*Slokuna*," he whispered.

Gee, which word should I use? The politically correct word or one of the many risqué ones? "Vagina," she whispered back. "It's also known as cunt, pussy, or Beth's pleasure palace." She giggled.

"What the hell are you doing?" Beth was mortified to hear Greta's voice. The headache pills must be working.

"Uh, oh—sorry, commander. I was just, um, helping Spike here, uh…"

"Never mind. I don't want to know. As an anthropologist, I'm assuming you're just doing research. But you'd better be careful—you might learn a lot more than you wanted to."

Embarrassed, Beth slipped away from the man. He cocked his head, his brow furrowing. He said something. There was an edge to his voice. Beth glanced down to see his penis tenting his loincloth.

"Uh, oh," Beth said. "I think I may have started something." She shook her head. Spike grabbed her and pulled her close, rubbing his erection against her.

"Oh, god. Get a room."

"Shit. I didn't mean to tease him like this, Commander. I was just trying to program the Ute—"

"Sure you were. And a very effective job you're doing, I can see. As mission commander, you know I'll have to report everything I observe." Beth blanched. Greta grinned, then covered her face with the cloth. "OK, I won't watch. But it's going to be harder not to listen, you know."

Beth was being pulled over to the man's bedding mat in one corner. "Oh, god, no!" How could she get herself into this situation? Had she secretly wanted to arouse him? Why else would she tease him?

There was something about this man she liked, she had to admit. He wasn't cruel like many of the others appeared to be. He was intelligent and curious, just like

Beth. And he was big. At 6-3, he towered over Beth's 5-4 frame. But this man clearly wanted her and didn't care if she carried a few extra pounds. That alone made her wet. Why shouldn't she get laid once in a while, even if it is with a being from another planet?

"OK, Commander, I'm only doing this in the interests of science," she breathed.

"I'm not list-en-ing," Greta sang out, her fingers in her ears.

Spike pulled her down roughly. She felt delicate in his arms. Beth tried to be at least somewhat objective in order to learn more about this sister race. When he pulled his loincloth aside, she studied his cock. Yes, it was very similar to human cocks. Bulbous head, thick shaft. And about a full size larger. She felt an urge to kiss it, but didn't know if that was the custom here. Instead, she stroked it gently, letting her fingers play up and down the large shaft, imagining it inside her. Suddenly, Beth felt herself becoming very wet.

Spike eased between her legs. She spread them almost eagerly. This man—this humanoid—wanted her! He had to have her. She wasn't going to deny him. Beth reached up and kissed him on the mouth. He smiled and kissed her back.

What do you know? Another human trait the species share!

She reached down and opened herself for him. She wanted him as much as he wanted her. *I haven't been laid in more than a year!* Still, it was risky, she knew. This species' sperm could be harmful to humans. There could be microbes we have no defense against. Even as these thoughts raced through her mind, Spike pressed his alien cock into her. It was a tight fit at first. He wiggled and pressed, even as her pussy gushed fluids to coat his enormous tool. It didn't take long before she felt his balls slap against her ass.

Beth widened her legs and sighed deeply. He filled her completely. "Size does matter," she whispered.

Spike pumped into her in earnest. He did not seem concerned for her pleasure, only his. Still, she was getting plenty from this close encounter of the third kind. Or maybe it's the fourth kind.

Beth felt an orgasm rapidly approaching. *How could this be? We're not supposed to be compatible.* Spike pulled her legs up over his shoulders, bending her almost in half. It allowed his cock to plunge deeper into her. The sensation was overpowering. Her orgasm was nearing, nearing. She began to make inarticulate noises in her throat. She didn't care if Greta could hear — in fact, she was no longer aware her commander was in the room.

He thrust hard and she felt his sperm squirt into her. The action triggered her own climax and she gasped and cried and shook all over as the emotions rocked her. "Sweet Jesus! Oh god!"

Thankfully, there was silence from Greta.

Spike pulled out and stood up. He said a few more words to her, then adjusted his loincloth and went to the water bucket for a drink. Beth was incapable of movement. She lay there, spread wide open, spent. She could feel his fluids leaking from her. *My god! I've just been fucked by an alien!*

When she was finally able to regain control of her limbs, she rolled over and sat up. More fluids gushed from her. She looked down, amazed. *The men on this planet come a gallon,* she observed. *No,* she said to herself. *Let's* be more scientific. Maybe it's just a quarter-cup. Still, it's a lot compared to mere Earth men.

Groggily, she got to her feet. Spike was saying something to her, pointing. She looked and saw a fireplace in the corner, same as at Lumpy's house. He mimed putting food in his mouth. *He wants me to cook after this experience?* God, some male characteristics are universal, she mused.

Beth dragged herself to the fire. The coals were still glowing from a previous meal, so it was easy for her to add some kindling to rekindle a flame. She added wood. Looking around, she wondered what kind of food they had on this planet. Beth was a good cook—but the food here might not be edible for an Earthling. At a minimum, it might taste bad

She opened a cabinet near the fireplace and rooted around. There was a half loaf of a dark bread. She sniffed it. It smelled vaguely like rye bread. A bowl contained some wilting vegetables, including what could pass for mushrooms. And wrapped in burlap there was a steak of some sort that smelled like it had been left too long in the sun. Beth wrinkled her nose.

"Oh, boy," she whispered, "roast beast."

Chapter 20

Kate Dyson was hot and thirsty. She had underestimated the amount of water she would need to walk thirty-five kilometers in this heat. It must be 110 degrees here. Trapped out on the plain, she was beginning to wonder if she would be able to make it.

She paused and slathered on more sunscreen. Her coveralls had proved to be far too hot for this environment, yet she hated to abandon them. Now she had them draped over her head like a turban, shielding her face from the unrelenting sun. Kate was dressed in her tee-shirt, bright pink panties and boots. She had taken off her bra a few miles back and buried it in the sand. Wouldn't want the natives to stumble across it. Might use it as a slingshot, she giggled. She knew the heat was beginning to affect her judgment.

She checked her scanner. She was still twenty-five klicks from the second pod, twenty-seven from the village. Kate shook her canteen. Just a few swallows left. There was no way she could walk all that way without water.

Kate studied the landscape, then held up the scanner to confirm her intuition. To her left the mountain ridge rose up five and a half kilometers away. The scanner told her there were water sources beyond the treeline. It would mean a detour that would add at least ten or twelve klicks to her trek. Yet she knew if she went straight on, she'd probably die before she reached her crew.

"That would do no good," she told herself. Sighing, Kate turned and headed east, toward the ridge.

* * * * *

Allyson stood as tall as her 5-6 frame would allow and tried to stare down the man who had purchased her. That was hard when she was getting a crick in her neck from looking up at him. He reminded her of that hotshot Chinese basketball player she'd been reading about on Earth, Chi Ming. He was seven feet tall as well.

"I'm not from this planet!" She shouted, trying to force him to understand. "Nor am I one of your bimbos! You must let me go!"

Almost casually, he backhanded her, knocking her to the floor. Ally lay there, dizzy, frustrated and angry. He said what she believed was the Devonite equivalent of a curse and spoke some angry words to the three women.

They were in a hotel of some sort, Ally believed. It was a large two-story log house, with several rooms. The man seemed to have purchased her to be a maid or a clerk. It wasn't clear what he was telling her. Ally could not fathom this language. And this man—Ming would do for a name, she thought—had no patience with women. He yelled at the three women who *could* understand him, so what chance did Ally have?

Ming strode away, muttering. The three native women gathered around Ally. One of them, a tall woman with a beak nose, cursed at her and kicked Ally in the side. A second one spoke a few harsh words to the first and pointed to the prostrate girl, then to the retreating back of their master. The third bent down and helped Ally up, talking soothing words to her. The first woman stalked off, trailed by the second.

The third woman had a round face, weathered with age. Her breasts hung down to her stomach. Ally tried to listen to the lilting language as she spoke, but could make no sense of it. "I don't understand," she said, shaking her head. "Please, help me. I want to know what you are saying."

Sighing, the woman led Ally to a courtyard and handed her a broom. It looked like something out of the "Wizard of Oz" — spindly branches tied to a stick. The woman pushed Ally into the yard and indicated that she should sweep. Crying, she stepped out into the hot sun and began moving the broom back and forth.

"I'm a fucking commander of a starship," she muttered. "Second in command to the captain! And here I am on this godforsaken planet, sweeping up dirt like a charwoman!"

* * * * *

Jorja was brought to the home of the father. Apparently, the young man lived there as well. It was an adobe hut with two rooms. A partially finished, smaller hut was right next door. The young man pushed her inside. The father and son began talking. Their voices seemed almost conspiratorial. They kept looking at her as if sizing her up.

The woman immediately went to the kitchen and started cooking. Once she stopped and came over with a drink of water for Jorja. The men paid her no attention. Jorja drank gratefully and thanked the woman as best she could.

The son — or Junior, as Jorja had begun to call him — came over and began talking to her, speaking slowly as if that would make her understand better. She just shook her head. "Look, asshole, I don't understand you. And if I was untied, I'd kick your butt again."

Her animosity came through. He stared at her for a moment, then turned back to his father, again speaking in that strange language.

What the hell were they plotting?

Chapter 21

Greta woke up the next morning feeling much better, she told the doctor. Beth was unable to attend to the commander because Spike had chained Beth up overnight on the bedding with him. He had fucked her again before they fell asleep—making love would be the wrong words for the animalistic coupling they enthusiastically performed. Her body had easily accommodated him this time. The feeling of his cock deep within her defied description. No sooner did he erupt within her and pull out then she wanted him again. She wanted to fall asleep with his hard cock grasped within her cunt. She had never felt that way with anyone before.

Beth was still embarrassed to be within earshot of her commander. And she was a little ashamed that she enjoyed it so much. For an older man, he sure did have stamina. And there was something about being chained up, naked, at the mercy of this love-making machine that secretly thrilled her.

I should probably have my head examined!

Now, in the gray light of dawn, Spike snored next to her. Greta had been left chained to the couch. To Beth, this meant that Spike had claimed her for his own. What he intended to do with Greta was a mystery. Beth was pleased to see that he had no interest in this slender, beautiful woman who made men drool back on Earth. *They like Reubenesque women on this planet, yippee!*

Spike woke up when he heard the women talking. He unlocked the chain and let Beth tend to Greta. She wetted the cloth and daubed the commander's head around the bandage.

"Oh, don't fuss over me any more, doc. I'm fine. My memory's coming back too."

"Good. I was worried about you. If we're going to sneak away, you'll have to be well enough to move under your own power. How's your knee?"

"It's better. I think I could walk a bit in a pinch."

"We may have to wait until you can run."

"We can't wait too long. We have to get back to that pod before the villagers trash it. First, we have to find where they've taken Smith and Egerton."

"I was hoping Spike here could help us," Beth said.

"Really? How so?"

"That depends on how well we can communicate with him."

"You think the Ute's ready?"

"I hope so. I wish Spike talked more. It's like pulling teeth to get him to say a few words."

"Sounds like my ex-husband. Where is it?"

"He has it. I think he still suspects it's some kind of trick. I know he's never seen anything like it."

"Can you ask him to check it?"

Beth nodded. "Let me get him something to eat first, put him in a good mood."

She went to the kitchen and cut a slice of bread, then slathered it with some preserves from a covered bowl on the counter. Spike, who had gone outside to pee, came in and smiled to see Beth being so obedient. She waited until he wolfed down his bread before signaling to him about the U.T. He nodded and pulled it out of his pouch.

The light glowed yellow.

"Commander! It's working! At least partially."

"Great. Tell him, um, tell him we're free women. No, that'll just make him mad. Tell him he has to let us go."

"Let's start with something small, hmm?" Beth wanted to build a relationship, not anger the man. Besides, the U.T. wasn't ready for any difficult words.

She mimed being allowed to hold the device. Spike reluctantly handed it over, ready to grab it back if she tried anything. Beth held it to her face and spoke into it. "My name is Beth Reyes. What is your name?"

The Ute repeated her words in the man's language with the characteristic pauses that indicated the computer was trying to fill in the blanks. His eyes widened and he stepped back. He said something the Ute couldn't translate. Beth was afraid it might be something like "Sorcery!"

"No, it's all right," she said, speaking carefully. She remembered her training with the U.T.s. You have to speak slowly and clearly and you can't use slang or idioms. "This machine lets me talk to you."

He nodded when the Ute translated. "I am Niktus, …[unknown] for the … [unknown]."

"What, um, tribe are you?"

"We are the Baktu. And you?"

Beth wasn't sure how much she dared tell him. "We come from a place called Earth."

"Yurth? Not heard of … [country-state]." Whenever it stuttered like that, Beth knew the machine was having a little trouble with some translations, so it gave two or three possibilities in rapid succession. She'd have to give it a little more time.

"It's far away from here. We were exploring when we were captured."

He nodded. "Why are women … [traveling-wandering] alone?"

"It is our custom. We are a free people."

The machine stuttered. "What is *freerl* people?"

Don't they have a word for free here? Or was the machine just slow on the learning curve?

"Here, men are free. They do what they want. Women are not free. They do what the men tell them to do."

"Ah. That is our way. Our women are … [cared-protected-loved]."

Beth thought of a dozen different arguments. She didn't want to get into philosophical discussion right now. Instead, she asked, "Why don't women wear clothes?"

"*Clorthes*? What *clorthes*?"

She pointed to his loincloth. "Clothes, like what you wear."

He laughed. "Not clothes. This is to keep penis from …[unknown] during work, causing pain."

"Don't women need to protect breasts during work?"

"No. Women don't work like men. Women need to show breasts, to attract [protector-master]."

"So women are, um, for sex only?"

Niktus shook his head. "*Serx*? What is *serx*?"

Great, the machine couldn't translate that yet, which meant she'd have to play charades. "Sex is what we you and I did—your penis and my vagina."

"Ahh, *nerhanka*. Not just sex. They work in house. Cook. Have [children-babies.] Help man."

Greta, listening to the exchange, groaned. "We've stumbled into a nightmare world, doc. We've gone back in time to when women were chattel. God help us—we've got to get out of here."

Beth quickly thumbed the Ute so it wouldn't translate her outburst. "Shh! It's not up to us to judge. This really isn't all that much different from our own 16th century, you know. Didn't you study your history?"

She snorted. "Anything before women got the right to vote and my eyes glazed over."

"Well, times were plenty tough on women back in our Middle Ages. Give the Baktu some time, they'll come around. Now, hang on while I sweet-talk this guy."

Beth thumbed the switch. "We don't belong here. We must return to our own people. Can you help us?"

Niktus shook his head. "Cannot undo sale. Can only sell again."

Beth flashed on a glimmer of an idea. "Can we buy ourselves back?"

"No. Only men have …[unknown] to buy, sell."

Greta couldn't help but speak up again. "Great. Just what Hunter had been warning about—if we'd taken a man along on this trip, maybe they would've let him buy us back."

"We'd never live that down," Beth retorted. To Niktus, she said, "We need to find our friends. We can help them talk to their new masters."

He nodded slowly. "Magic box helps."

"Do you know everyone who bought women of my tribe?"

"Yes."

"Can you take me to them?"

Niktus pursed his lips, thinking. "They will want box too."

"That man has them. The one who brought us in. Gorshun?"

"Gorshun. Yes. He will want much coin for box when he know what it do." He smiled. "I buy first."

Beth couldn't help but smile as well. Niktus was a true capitalist. Wait until he found out what the medical kit could do.

Chapter 22

Kate walked the last two klicks without a drop of water. The heat bore down until she felt like an ant under a magnifying glass. She could see the trees ahead, yet they shimmered and danced away each time she thought she was close. Kate carried only the small backpack containing the scanner, her phaser, Ute, the explosives, food, and the empty canteen. Her coveralls had been left somewhere back — she hadn't had the energy to bury them. Some native will start wearing those and be crowned king, she thought, almost giddy. More meddling in their affairs. It mattered little now.

Her legs were on autopilot, one sliding in front of the other, knees wobbling. To stop would mean failure and that one thought drove Kate onward above all others. She wasn't going to leave her crew trapped on this planet. *Everyone's going back*, she kept telling herself. *Everyone's going back.*

The trees swayed in front of her. She was used to their tricks by now. Any minute now the optical illusion would shatter and she'd be faced with another kilometer of open plain, the heat sapping the fluids from her exhausted body. Kate tripped and sprawled down. She lay there, crying softly without any tears, trying to find the energy to get up again.

Her outstretched hand touched something rough. She expected a rock, but it wasn't. Groggily, she looked up to see her hand resting at the base of a spindly tree. Kate looked around and saw more trees. She had made it to the treeline.

Shade!

Crawling now, she moved into the embrace of the trees, feeling the harsh sunlight thwarted in its efforts to burn her alive. She lay there for several minutes, letting the shade refresh her. Finally, the urgent signals from her brain reached her exhausted limbs — *Water! You need water!*

Groaning, she rolled the backpack off one shoulder and fumbled for the scanner. Holding it up, she checked for the nearest water source. Just one-half kilometer away. Without the sun flattening her, Kate thought she just might make it. Using a branch for support, she pulled herself upright and staggered on.

She no longer trusted her judgment or her sense of direction. Keeping the scanner in one hand, she moved through the trees like a pinball through a game, bouncing from one tree to another, always moving toward her goal. Kate felt the branches rip at her tee-shirt. She knew she was close now — she could smell moisture in the air. It was like a drug, invigorating her, intoxicating her. Kate came over the top of a ravine and looked down to a beautiful sight — a shallow stream, maybe ten feet wide, sluggishly moving through an ancient streambed.

Her mouth open in anticipation, Kate stumbled down the slope, dropped her backpack and scanner and flopped headlong into the lukewarm, delicious water. She didn't care if it contained microbes or deadly parasites. She would have to take that chance. It was her salvation and she welcomed it. She drank and drank until her stomach hurt.

She lay a long time in the water, her face turned to the side to suck air. Her clothes — what little she had on — were soaked and she didn't mind a bit. Finally, she dragged herself back to the shore. She sat under the shade of a large tree and thanked the stars that she had been given this reprieve. The idea of leaving this tiny paradise and walking back across the plain to the village was too painful to think about for the moment.

Kate picked up the scanner and checked her position. She was now thirty-one kilometers from the village. Her best route would be to travel south for about twenty-six klicks, staying close to water, then cut across the plain. She would pass by the pod and be able to check on its condition. For now, however, a rest was in order. She lay back her head and dozed.

She wasn't sure how long she had been asleep when a noise startled her. Instantly she was alert, her hand dipping into her backpack to grasp her phaser. She looked up, trying to trace the source of the noise. Her eyes focused on the opposite bank. She sat up quickly, sucking in her breath.

A native woman was standing there, staring across the stream at her, a frightened look on her face. Perhaps she had come down for a drink and had seen the sleeping captain. The woman wasn't naked like all the others Kate had seen from the photos. This one was wearing an animal skin that covered her breasts and another one wrapped around her waist. She was heavy-set, dark and hairy.

Kate wanted to run but felt paralyzed. The woman said something. Her odd language triggered Kate's brain into action. She slipped her hand off of the pistol and found the Ute. She flicked the switch on the side. The woman repeated her call, but made no attempt to cross the stream.

The captain knew she was still too weak to escape. If the woman was traveling with men, Kate would have to fight her way out. Her hand found the reassuring butt of her phaser again and waited.

The woman turned and called out. From the trees came two other women, dressed similarly to the first. They stopped when they spotted the strange woman. Another one called out to Kate. This time, she felt she couldn't ignore them.

"I'm sorry. I don't understand you," she said. "As you can see, I'm not from around here."

Her language floored the three women. Their voices were raised and in minutes, four other women came out of the trees. No men. That was strange. They not only stared at Kate, but they also looked in the trees up and down the river, as if expecting a trap.

That gave Kate a little hope. It was possible they might share the same enemy—the men who kidnapped her crew. She decided to try a little experiment.

Slowly, she stood and came closer to the edge of the stream, carrying her backpack with her. The women jabbered and backed up. *Aha!* They were more afraid of her than she was of them. Of course, if she were unarmed, she'd be terrified too.

"It's OK," she said, taking her hand out of her backpack and holding both arms up. "I come in peace." *I've always wanted to say that.*

Now what? she wondered. Kate hesitated to cross the stream. Being surrounded by these women—all of whom seemed taller than her—would be intimidating. Certainly, they'd want to touch her, to feel her smooth skin and pluck at her strange clothes. They might try to grab her pack.

Kate knew it was all about attitude. If she acted afraid, they'd be superior. If she acted like the captain she was, however...

She squared her shoulders and waded across the stream. The women scattered. Some ran back into the trees, others fled up and down the water's edge. Kate stopped moving immediately. She waited until they began creeping back toward her.

"It's OK," she said again. "Talk to me. My Ute needs to hear you."

Cautiously, they came closer. One woman seemed braver than the rest and approached Kate. She stood about two inches taller than the captain. Her animal skins were adorned with shells that had been tied on with thin strips of bark. On her head, she wore some sort of helmet made out of sections of thick tree bark. It made her look medieval.

She spoke in that strange language. Kate shook her head, then shrugged. She didn't even know if her gestures meant the same thing here. *At least it's a start.*

Another idea occurred to her. She put her hand up to her mouth, feigning hunger. She had food in her pack, but if she could pretend to be lost and hungry, they might sit down with her long enough for the Ute to learn their language.

The woman slowly nodded. She stepped aside and indicated that Kate should accompany them. Kate fell in behind her and the group of women followed. They wound their way through the trees for about a kilometer until they came to a clearing. A firepit was set up in the center, surrounded by lean-tos. There were more women here. Again, no men.

Were they hiding out from the slave traders?

When they spotted Kate, their voices were raised, some in alarm. They surrounded her. As she had expected, they touched her clothes, brushed their hands over her smooth skin. When someone pulled at her backpack, she recoiled and said, "Don't touch that!"

The shell woman spoke up and the women backed off. Kate nodded to herself—the woman was the leader. She wanted to learn her name. Kate got her attention. Patting her chest, she said, "Kate." Then she reached out to her. "What's your name?"

The woman nodded once and said, "*Sulala.*"

"*Sulala,*" Kate repeated, nodding. "It's very nice to meet you."

Sulala said a few words to two of the women and they scampered off toward one of the lean-tos. She indicated that Kate should sit near the fire. After the searing heat of the plain, the last thing she needed was a fire, but to be polite, she sat, albeit as far away from the flames as possible.

"Fire," she said, pointing.

"*Hobatt,*" the woman said.

Kate reached into her backpack and found the Ute. Careful not to let them see it, she pressed the button to record the equivalencies. "Fire, *Hobatt,*" she repeated. She and Sulala identified three other nouns and programmed them before the two women returned with food.

It was a meager meal. Mostly roots, berries and nuts. There were two bites of a dried meat of unknown origin. It supported her theory. The women were hiding out and they weren't having much success hunting for food. Kate was savvy enough to know that while for her this could only be considered a snack, to these women, they were presenting her with a banquet. She expressed tremendous gratitude and ate sparingly. She wanted to share some of her pouches of food, but decided to wait. They may not understand why she asked for food when she had some with her.

After she ate, the women seemed to relax a bit. They sat around, chatting to each other, trying to share words with Kate and have some successes. Each time she found an equivalent, she dutifully recorded it into her U.T.

The women eyed her backpack. They were clearly curious to find out what was in it—and why Kate kept reaching into it. After nearly an hour, when their feeble attempts at conversation dragged, Kate decided to show them. She retrieved the Ute from her pack and held it up. The women shrank back, confused.

"No, it's all right," she assured them. She checked the device. The display light glowed yellow. *Thank god!* She thumbed the response switch.

"My name is Kate." The UT spoke her words in their language. Several of the women screamed, some fled. Only Sulala remained quiet, although she appeared distressed.

"I mean you no harm. This box will help us talk. You may speak now."

Sulala opened, then closed her mouth. Kate hoped the Ute was able to convey her message. Finally, she said, "What ... [unknown] is this?"

She guessed what the Ute had failed to translate. "It's not magic," Kate said. "It is a common tool in my country.

We use it to talk to new people we meet. Like you." She indicated all of them. They began drifting back.

"You are ... [traveler-lost]?"

Kate nodded. "Yes, from land far away. There are others like me here. They got lost. I must find them."

"Where did you lose them?"

"In village." She pointed southwest. The mention of the village frightened the women.

"Many ... [enemies-opponents] in *Lakapit*."

"I know. My friends are held captive. I must get them."

Sulala shook her head. "Can not do. Men will take you."

Kate looked her in the eye. "I must. I am, um, in charge of them."

"They say only men are in charge. Women are [slaves-captives]."

The captain sensed she was being tested. "I don't agree," she said gently. "Neither do you. That is why you stay in forest."

"Yes. We will not be bought and sold. We are free people. We call ourselves *Bakchari*."

"You are brave women, you *Bakchari*. There are many women like you in my country. Do you plan to stay in forest?"

"For now," she said. "Enemies many. Strong. We are few. Slave traders come and raid us. We run, hide."

Kate wished there was something she could do for these women. They would just have to work it out themselves, just like women on Earth did over the centuries. That didn't make her feel any better.

"Can you help me reach the village? I must travel through forest, stay hidden from men."

"Yes. I take you to *Lakapit*. *Lilani* go as well. But not today. Darkness come soon."

"All right. Tomorrow."

Chapter 23

Beth watched, quietly holding her breath, as Niktus bargained hard with Gorshun for the remaining three U.T.s. Once she had them, she could use the first one to program the others in minutes via infrared link. Then Ally and Jorja could communicate with their owners and perhaps they could all figure a way out of this mess.

Gorshun, Beth knew, would want to know why Niktus was so interested in these mysterious boxes that didn't appear to do anything. During her talks with the man, Beth learned he was considered a healer in the village. His treatments consisted of herb teas, setting bones and bleeding for fevers—not all that dissimilar from Earth four centuries ago.

Before they arrived at Gorshun's hut, Beth suggested Niktus tell him that the strange women needed the devices to remain healthy in this country's heat. Niktus agreed that would strike fear into the slave trader. "He wouldn't want to have customers coming back, demanding a refund!" he laughed.

The ruse worked. Niktus and Beth left with the Utes, and grinned all the way back to his house. Inside, she quickly programmed the devices. Then she handed two of them over. The third she saved for Greta.

"Go make some profit," she said. He nodded, a smile creasing his face.

Beth was really beginning to like this alien.

* * * * *

Jorja looked up from her bedding to see a strange man standing over her. She sat up quickly, her collar chain clinking, and spotted Junior and his father behind him. The newcomer stood about six-four—somewhat short by this race's standards—but was broad in the chest and had powerful arms and legs. Jorja couldn't help but think he was pretty good-looking for an alien.

He spoke to her, several sentences. Jorja just shrugged and said, "Sorry, pal, I don't understand you. But if you were inviting me out for a dinner and a movie, I'd probably say yes."

The man turned and spoke a few harsh sentences to the other men. The older man said something in reply that apparently angered this man. He responded curtly and started to leave.

The door opened suddenly and an older man Jorja didn't recognize came in, followed by—Beth!

"Beth! Thank god! I wondered what happened to you and the others!"

"Jorja! I'm glad you're all right. We've got Utes!" the doctor replied. "We can talk now."

Niktus spoke to the owners for a few minutes. The stranger just watched, his face set. Niktus turned on one of the devices and spoke to Jorja. "Slave, stand up."

"Fuck y—" She started to say.

"For god's sakes, Jorja, just do what he says. He's trying to make a sale here," Beth said, exasperated.

Swallowing her pride, Jorja stood. The other three men appeared stunned.

"Now, lift one leg."

Jorja stared at Beth. "He's kidding, right?"

"Please, Jorja!"

The engineer reluctantly complied, then put her leg down again almost immediately. The men began talking among themselves, so fast the Ute could barely keep up.

"Amazing!"

" —never seen anything—"

" —means we can train her." The last came from the newcomer.

Jorja didn't like what she was hearing. "OK, we can all understand each other. So understand this: I'm not a slave. None of us are. We come from another, uh, country, where women are free. You must release us."

"I'm afraid it's not that simple, Jorja," Beth put in. "This entire culture is based on the enslavement of women. They can't conceive of letting us go."

"We have to try, doc!"

"I know. It may take a little time to figure something out."

Niktus cut Beth off with a wave of his hand. To the men, he said. "You have seen how the magic boxes work. Everyone who owns strange slave should have one until she learns our language."

The men nodded. The bargaining began. Beth didn't know their monetary system here, but it was clear from Niktus' pleased expression that he made a good profit.

Beth and Niktus turned to go. "Wait! You're not going to leave me here with these guys!"

"I'm sorry, Jorja. We have to go find the man who bought Ally. We'll be back, I promise. For now, at least you can talk to them."

With that, they left. When the door slapped shut on Beth, Jorja felt abandoned all over again. Still, at least she had hope. *If anyone can figure out these people, it's Beth.*

"I am Dolnark," the older man said. "This is my son, Gulnark. This man is trainer, Keltar."

"I am Jorja Smith of the free nation of Earth." She didn't dare tell them Earth was another planet.

"Yes, but you are here now. I own you," Dolnark said. "I have given you to my son."

"And I must be satisfied," put in the younger man. "You must be punished for what you did."

"In our country, we don't allow men to mate with us on street corners," Jorja huffed.

"You are not in your country," Gulnark pointed out. "Now it is time for you to earn profit. If not, you shall be punished."

Before Jorja could respond, Keltar grabbed her upper arm. "Slave, it is time to go." he said. Gulnark stepped forward to unlock her collar chain.

"Go? Go where?"

"To the training area. To prepare."

"Prepare for what?" Jorja looked at the other two men. They had Chesire cat grins on their faces.

"You are big fighter, hurt my son," the older man said. "Now we make money from you. You go with Keltar. He train you for *jamkalut.*"

The Ute didn't have an equivalent word. "What is *jamkalut*?" She asked.

Keltar smiled. "Fight. Contest. Much fun."

Jorja paled. "You're going to put me in a ring with another poor girl and make us fight?"

The men all laughed when the translation was made clear. "No, no," Keltar said. "You fight man."

As the men explained it in more detail, Jorja began shaking her head. Apparently, for entertainment, the men held matches of some sort in the public square. Villagers turned out and bet on the outcomes. The fighters were all hardened men, well trained and probably deadly.

"There's no way I'm going to do that," she said. "Even if I did, I'd be killed. I can't fight one of these huge guys."

"No choice," Dolnark said. "You hurt my son in front of villagers. He earned revenge. You fight, or you suffer punishments."

"Then I'll…" She trailed off. She couldn't let them beat her like a dog! "What happens if I win? Will I be allowed to go home?"

"No. But my son will feel better about losing to slave. If you can beat fighter, you can beat many man in village."

"I am sure we will have many fine matches in future," Keltar put in.

"Well, forget it, boys. I'm not going to fight. The man will win and your son will look like a wimp."

There were some puzzled looks. Apparently, "wimp" did not translate well. Jorja didn't care.

"If you refuse to fight, then maybe another Earth woman can be made to fight," Gulnark said, smirking. "Perhaps the light-haired one."

Jorja knew he meant Greta. "You bastard! I'll kick your ass all over again!" She lunged at him, but Keltar hauled her back by her arm. The father and Keltar laughed when Gulnark shrunk back. His face darkened over the embarrassment.

Jorja turned and tried to knock the man's grip loose, but he parried her blows easily. "You have strength, speed. It will be a pleasure to ready you."

"Do you think she'll be ready by *Dulston's* matches?" Gulnark asked.

Keltar shrugged. "Can not say now. Will have to study her. Never heard of a slave fight before."

"Who will she be matched against?"

"Don't know. Ask me tomorrow. Now, let me have magic box so I can train her."

Gulnark reluctantly handed it over. "You take good care of that. It's worth many *quitnums.*"

Keltar just nodded, snapped his leash onto Jorja's collar and dragged her out. As much as she wanted to be away from the old man and his son, she was more afraid of this brooding, taciturn trainer.

Once they were outside, he surprised her by smiling at her. "If what villagers say is true, we make good profit."

Escorting her to the cart, she was further amazed to be allowed to ride up front. "I didn't think slaves rode up here," she commented.

"They do not. Will make villagers talk. They know who I am. They will wonder about you."

Jorja couldn't help but laugh. "In our country, it would be called marketing."'

The joke was lost on Keltar. "I did not see what you did to Gulnark, and I am sorry I missed it. That boy needed a lesson. To have a slave beat him up!" He guffawed loudly.

"You don't like him?"

"No. He is braggart. His father is village elder, so son does what he please. No good."

Jorja smiled. Finally! Someone who agreed with her. "Why is he making me fight stranger? Why not try to fight me himself?"

Keltar laughed again. "Good point! I think he is afraid of you. He is already embarrassed. Can not bear to lose twice, so he calls for substitute. But I think I know his strategy. He will bet on you to lose, and hope you win."

Jorja was confused. "I don't understand."

"If you win, it will show village that he is not weak, that good fighter could not beat you. If you lose, he makes profit."

Ahh, she thought. That makes sense. These people loved a profit. "The way women are treated in this village, it's a wonder anyone will bet on me to win."

"True. But many people watched your fight with the boy. Even now, word is going from house to house. By the time match comes up, you could be big hero, very strong fighter."

"What if I bet on myself to win—can I win my freedom back, along with the other women of my tribe?"

"Maybe. If you had a man to make bids for you. If a man make enough money on match." He slapped the reins on the donkey's back. "For now, I want to see what magic you have in arena."

Chapter 24

Allyson strained against her ropes, cursing and struggling. The coarse hemp cut into her wrists and ankles. She screamed into the gag covering her mouth. She had been forced by the huge man over this padded sawhorse-like structure that he set up in the hotel lobby, her arms and legs tied to the supports. She was mortified to be bent over and spread out like this, her ass and cleft exposed to any visitors who came in.

Apparently, she was some sort of perk for the man's guests. He was retaliating for her obstinate refusal to do her chores in a matter befitting a slave. The starship commander would rather die than clean latrines and sweep courtyards. However, this indignity was far worse.

Fortunately for Ally, business was slow this time of day. So far, only one man had checked in, two slaves in tow, and he was too tired to partake of the manager's kind invitation to relieve his stress with the bound woman. Instead, he merely spanked her sharply a few times on her bare ass and let it go at that. The hotel owner laughed at her discomfort as she squirmed under the man's blows.

So she was still waiting for her first real "customer" when Niktus walked in with Beth mid-afternoon. Beth gasped when she saw her commander. "Oh my god, Commander Egerton! Hang on, I'll try to get you out of there."

She whispered a few words to Niktus, holding the Ute close so the brooding hotel manager couldn't hear. Niktus nodded and said, "I will speak to him."

They approached the desk. "Greetings, *Pitus*! How is business?"

"Good, Niktus, good. I see you are out with your slave today—I hope she is more obedient than mine! What a difficult slave!"

"Yes. But let me tell you, Pitus, these slaves are very unusual. I can see you are trying to discipline her, I just hope you do not ruin her value while you do it."

"What do you mean?"

"Did you not hear about the big one they captured and sold to Dolnark?"

"Yes, I did hear that. She attacked his son—most distressing."

"That is my point. Where have you heard of a slave attacking a man—not only that, but knocking him to the ground twice!"

"It is odd. I heard Dolnark has given her to Keltar to train for a *jamkalut* in two suns time."

"It is true. She and one of Keltar's fighters will match before the big Klasdor-Ripatus fight to warm up the crowd. I hear she is good fighter."

He snorted. "I will have to see."

"This woman is from same tribe," Niktus said, pointing at the bent-over Ally. "They are not easily tamed. I do not think they would make good hotel slaves."

"I paid good money for her, I use her as I see fit."

"Of course." Niktus stepped close and allowed his hand to rest on Ally's naked ass. She flinched, as if trying to get away. He stroked her as he continued to speak to Pitus. "But as you yourself have seen, these are exotic creatures, not at all like the hairy slaves we are used to."

He rubbed his hands over her, letting his fingers stray into her cleft, drawing juices from her against her will. A groan slipped from her lips into her gag. "Yes, they are highly sexual women—I can tell you from my own experience with my slave here." Beth blushed. "But they have many more qualities that you have not been able to determine."

His fingers worked into her slit, finding her clit and rubbing it gently. Ally couldn't help but be aroused. She told herself it was because she hadn't had sex in several months, but she knew being exposed here like this was incredibly erotic, despite—or maybe because of—her acute embarrassment.

Pitus moved closer as well in order to observe the heated woman writhe against her bonds. Beth was embarrassed, but she couldn't take her eyes off the scene. She was grateful that Ally couldn't see her from her bent-over position.

Niktus's fingers were soon coated in Ally's juices. Pitus sniffed at the pungent odor and made some comment Beth didn't catch. Both men laughed. Niktus pulled away and tasted his fingertips. Pitus dipped a finger in as well for a taste. Beth could see both men were becoming aroused—their loincloths stretched against their erections. Niktus returned his hand to Ally's cleft and continued to rub her.

Ally, a prisoner of her own body's arousal, wanted Niktus to stop—and she wanted him to continue. She was embarrassed, she was turned on. Her clit thrummed with need. His fingers felt so good, so good. Yes, that's it, please, please...

Suddenly, she spasmed and groaned softly, as if she was trying to hide her climax, though it was obvious to all.

"You can see how responsive she is and you tie her up like a common slave. Of course, I cannot blame you for not knowing. How could you? You cannot even talk to her."

Niktus segwayed cleanly into his sales pitch, taking the Ute from Beth and turning up the volume so the man could hear. Pitus jerked back when it spoke in a strange language, but when Beth spoke a few words and it translated for her, he began to see the possibilities.

He removed Ally's gag. The commander hung limply, lost in her euphoria. Then she seemed to come to her senses as her embarrassment and anger returned. Pitus held the machine close to her mouth and told her to speak. "Untie me you damned asshole!" the commander spit out. "I don't care if you are a giant, I'll rip your balls off!"

"See? You would never get such vile curses and demands from a Baktu woman after bringing her such pleasure. These slaves are different. I tell you, Pitus, this woman may make you a fortune if you stop trying to treat her as an ordinary slave."

Pitus was intrigued, although he didn't quite follow what Niktus was saying. "She could stand some manners. Being the guest greeter works wonders with most slaves—what else could she do for me?"

"My slave tells me she is good with numbers. Perhaps she could help you increase your profits."

"A slave who can add and subtract? Impossible!"

"Do not take my word for it. See for yourself—if you can talk to her."

Niktus quickly sold the Ute to the manager, then left him, studying the box and Ally's backside. Beth wanted to see her released, afraid that the big man would rape Ally after they left. That possibility didn't concern Niktus. But he assured her that Pitus would release her soon enough.

"You cannot order a Baktu man to do anything," he said. "You can only suggest that it is unprofitable and hope that he agrees with you."

The more Beth learned about this race, the more intrigued she became.

Chapter 25

Jorja was escorted into a large courtyard. At one end, an adobe structure filled about a third of the space.

"These are the barracks. Because we've never had a woman before, you will stay in my quarters," Keltar was saying.

When Jorja whipped around to eyeball him, he held up his hands. "Relax," he said quickly. "You belong to another man. I could face sanctions if I made sex with you. I might even lose my training business."

She relaxed then. Keltar introduced her to some of the fighters, who were practicing in the yard. Some of the men were huge. They just stared at her, not able to fathom a woman wanting to be a fighter. One young man laughed, then caught himself when he saw the trainer was serious. Keltar explained that Jorja was the woman who had beaten Gulnark. She could see a glimmer of understanding come into their eyes.

Keltar gave an order to one of the men and he jogged off.

"I thought we would start by letting you observe our fighting style in *jamkalut*," he said. "Then you can tell me if you feel you can defeat anyone."

Jorja watched two men square off. The Baktu fought with a combination of boxing and wrestling, she noted. They punched or grappled with their hands and only occasionally did they try to use their feet to trip their opponents. She began to see flaws in their technique. Not many, but flaws nevertheless. She might be able to exploit them, if she could stay on her feet against a bigger, more powerful opponent.

The man came back with some leather gear. Keltar handed Jorja some padded leather gloves. Not boxing gloves. More like karate gloves, which had padding only along the knuckles. She felt very comfortable with them. A leather helmet, padded near her temples, protected her head.

"Um, Keltar. Do you have anything I can wear to protect my breasts and groin?"

"Ahh. Of course." He barked out another order and the man ran off again. He returned with some wrappings of animal skins. For the first time since she had been captured, Jorja was able to cover herself. Immediately, she felt better.

"Can I borrow those extra gloves? I'd like to put them on my feet."

He looked puzzled. "Feet? Why you need protection on feet?"

"I'll show you." She put them on over her instep, and tied the straps as best she could. Jorja stretched out for a few minutes with some leg splits and jogging in place. When she was ready, she asked Keltar to hold up his hand, head-high. He cocked his head and complied, his hand out, palm flat. The other fighters turned to look at the strange behavior.

Jorja stood before him, right leg forward, motionless. Then with a sudden movement, she kicked up high and slapped the palm of his hand with the padded edge of her foot. It sounded like a gunshot in the quiet courtyard.

Keltar's mouth fell open. He shook the sting out of his hand. "*Jumulat!*"

"I can't kick any higher," she said. "If I'm pitted against a big man, I'll probably lose."

He waved his hand. "I have not decided who you will fight. Gulnark left it to me. Depends on the betting. If you are the underdog, we will pair you against a lesser opponent and my agents will bet on you. If the gossip about your fight with Gulnark has made you invincible, I'll put you up against a good fighter and let you lose."

Jorja was shocked. "Sounds like cheating!"

"Cheating? What is cheating?"

When Jorja explained, he laughed. "We call that 'controlling profits.' It is honorable business. Secret is to guess which way fight will go. Now, you try small fight. *Parmus?*"

A man stepped from the group of fighters. He was slender, about three inches taller than Jorja—a worrisome height, to be sure, but she could manage. Keltar made him put on gloves and helmet. "Take it slow," he warned the big man. "She is valuable. Much profit."

They circled each other. Jorja watched for openings, weaknesses. He expected an easy victory, yet he was being overly cautious until his pals began taunting him.

"Go, go, what are you afraid of?"

"Letting the girl frighten you, Parmus?"

Their goading made him rash. He lunged and tried to grab her upper arm. She blocked him, stepped to the side and kicked him hard in the solar plexus. The wind exploded out of him. She pulled at his arm, then stepped in and jammed her right foot behind his knee, knocking him to a kneeling position. Then she whipped the leg around and caught him on the back of the head with her foot, knocking him to the dust.

The other fighters' taunts ceased as if they had all suddenly lost their ability to speak. Parmus scrambled up immediately, embarrassment coloring his face. "Not fair!" He shouted. "She kicks!"

"How else do you expect me to keep up with you?" She responded. "You're taller, you outweigh me—I need my kicks just to survive."

"Hmm. I agree. That's how you defeated Gulnark. We will call fight as a 'no-rules' match. I do not want you to change anything. The crowd will go wild over you," Keltar said, smiling. "I am going to make a fortune."

"Don't you mean *we are* going to make a fortune?" Jorja wanted to make sure she would be included in the profits, otherwise, there would be no reason to fight. She had to make enough to free her crew.

"Women do not need …," he started to say, then stopped. "We can work out deal. Meanwhile, let us go again."

Jorja fought two others before she was too exhausted to continue. One of the men had been six-six and weighed more than 250 pounds. He was able to plow right through her kicks and knock her to the ground time and again. He was just too big. Keltar took note of this and told her he'd make sure her opponents were 'short fighters' of six-two or -three.

She pulled out all the stops to impress the trainer, anxious to have him make bets on her behalf so she might buy her friends back. She hadn't thought it all the way through yet, but she was working on it.

* * * * *

It took all day to hike thirteen kilometers south through the forest. Kate was grateful for the company of Sulala and Lilani. Before they started, Sulala suggested Kate ditch the torn white tee-shirt and don native animal skins, to better blend into the forest. That advice may have saved her from being spotted by a pair of slave traders. Crouching behind some trees, watching the slavers' cart move along the narrow trail, Kate was glad she had listened. Her white shirt would've been like a beacon against the green forest.

As they walked, Kate learned quite a bit about the women on this planet. Some women objected to their status, but few did anything about it. It was just the way things were. The men maintained firm control of the village leaderships. Any suggestions that women be given more control over their lives were always shot down by those in charge. It was a real Catch-22 for the women. They couldn't become elders, so they couldn't change policies that would allow them to become elders.

Not all women objected, of course. Many had loving masters, who treated them well and encouraged them to excel in areas that were traditionally female, such as cooking, raising children, or craftwork. Others objected to this narrow definition of their lives and tried to rebel in whatever way they could.

Sulala had the misfortune to be owned by a cruel master, which led to her revolt. One day, after a particularly bad beating for a minor infraction, Sulala managed to free herself later that night and run for the safety of the forest. Her "husband" or "master" — the words appeared to be interchangeable in the Baktu language—looked for her for a while, then gave up and bought a new slave.

When Sulala first arrived, there were just a handful of women in the forest, all living in fear—fear of staying in the forbidding woods and fear of returning home to abuse. They were disorganized, starving and demoralized. Sulala had the idea that there was strength in numbers. Through friends, she sent secret messages back to her village and those nearby, letting women know that there was an alternative to enduring bad masters. Soon, others filtered into the woods, finding the ragtag group, adding strength and talents to their camp.

Food was still a problem, however. Few of the women had learned to hunt effectively, so their efforts weren't as successful as they had hoped. But they were learning. Kate was so moved by this that she vowed to zap a beast for them if she had the chance, and to hell with the Prime Directive.

It was slow going in the forest. It would have been far easier if they could come out to the edge of the plain and travel without obstacles. Of course, that would have exposed them to the slavers. They stayed to the trails unless they caught wind of an approaching traveler, then crept off to hide out until they could see who was approaching. Once it had been a single woman who had recently fled her master. She sobbed when she saw Sulala, knowing that she had found the *Bakchari* at last. The chief took her aside and greeted her quietly, then told her how to find the others back up the trail.

They camped off the trail, deeper into the woods. Sulala risked a small fire. They had only nuts and berries to eat until Kate said she was going hunting and left them by the fire as dusk approached. They had wanted to go with her. Kate told them she hunted better on her own. She crept through the forest until she found another small mammal and shot it with her phaser. When she returned, they were surprised at her success.

"Are you sure you do not want to join our camp?" Sulala asked. "We could use a skilled hunter."

"I would very much like that, but I have to find my friends and return to our homeland," Kate said.

Lilani skinned and cooked the beast. It was delicious. Tasted just like pork, Kate decided. Or maybe chicken. Thus sated, they agreed on a watch schedule and went to sleep. When it was Kate's turn to keep watch, she sat with her scanner and gauged distances and tried to figure out what she would do to rescue her crew. She had a glimmer of a plan, now it was time to flesh it out. She sat there in the darkness, illuminated only by the glowing coals from the fire, and added details until she thought she just might stand a chance.

Chapter 26

Beth was changing her opinion of these people. When she first was captured, she felt the men were incredibly cruel toward women and the women were far too submissive for their own good. But living with Niktus and observing him, she could see women had more power here than she first thought. It all depended upon the man.

Niktus was a good man. He remained dominant, to be sure, because that was his nature. Still, he listened to Beth and took her advice on occasion. He knew she was smart and her race surpassed his own—the Utes and the other strange devices they had carried made that clear.

He also proved to be an incredible lover. Their couplings occurred morning and night. Hot, lusty sex like Beth had never experienced before. She couldn't get enough of him. Beth had long since stopped worrying about what Greta might think of her actions. Greta even indicated she was a bit jealous of all the good lovin' that was going on under her nose.

"Maybe when I recover, you'll share him, hmmm?" She asked. Beth wasn't sure if she was kidding or not.

When Beth told Niktus that she was a healer like him and the medical kit Gorshun had could help cure a lot of illnesses in the village, he became determined to buy it. He saw it as a way to increase his profits. The fact that it allowed Beth to do the job she had been trained to do was of secondary importance. She realized that profits were the men's great weakness. They could be convinced to do many things if a good profit appeared at the end of it. She suspected the women here would know that too. Perhaps being a woman on this planet isn't so bleak after all.

Niktus had gone alone to Gorshun's hut, leaving Beth and Greta unchained for the first time. Niktus wasn't overly concerned they might run away. He warned them that slaves were not permitted outside without a man present, otherwise, they might risk being declared "available" and claimed by another man. This was how many a cruel and unscrupulous master gained new slaves.

Greta and Beth decided not to risk it without well-thought-out plan. They sat and plotted how they might get away, inventing and rejecting various scenarios. The best idea was to steal the phasers and hide them. Then, at night, they could sneak to the houses of the other crew women and free them. Once they were all together, they may be able to blast their way free.

"If we're going to be sneaking around anyway, we should sneak over to Gorshun's and steal the whole bag," Greta said. "As you know, we can't leave *anything* behind."

"True. Maybe we can get Niktus to help us. Otherwise, I don't know how we're going to slip away."

"We could jump him and tie him up tonight."

"No way. He's been good to us."

"Yes, I've noticed how good he is to *you*."

Greta's emphasis made Beth blush. "I can't help what he does," she said hurriedly.

"It's OK," Greta assured her. "I think he's kinda cute myself."

Beth was trying to come up with a retort when Niktus entered the hut. One look at his face and Beth knew something was up.

"What is wrong, Master Niktus?" She asked, using the formal title.

"I bought the potions box," he began.

"Oh, that's wonderful!" Beth responded, then stopped when his face didn't reflect her excitement. His eyes shifted over to the commander.

"Uh oh," Greta said.

Beth's hand flew to her face. "You didn't!"

"It was the only way he would make a deal. He was angry when he discovered how valuable the talking boxes were. He said he would only accept Greta back as payment."

"Tell him no!" Beth blurted out. "He can't have her!"

"Beth," he said, pronouncing it "Beeth," "you know I only bought Greta because I thought I could make a larger profit later, when she got better. A trade with Gorshun is fair. This box of potions will help us as healers."

"No!—" Beth was just getting a head of steam up when Greta put her hand on her shoulder.

"It's all right, doc." Greta said, shocking Beth. To Niktus, she said, "May I speak to her alone?" He nodded.

"Kill the U.T.," she told Beth, who pressed the button to mute the unit.

"You can't possibly want to do this," Beth said.

"No, listen. Our plan relies on us getting the bag—or at least the phasers. If I'm there, I'll have a much better chance of doing that. Besides, I'm kinda the third wheel here, if you know what I mean."

Beth reddened again. Yet what she said made sense. She didn't like it, but if they were to escape and get back to the pod, they had to work fast—and smart. Finally, she nodded. "OK. You're right. But I don't like the look of that Gorshun. He could be a real bastard."

"I hope I'm not there long enough to find out," Greta said. She was thinking something else entirely. Being around Niktus and Beth, listening to their wild couplings, made Greta envious. If she got laid while on her mission to recover the phasers, well, it was a small sacrifice to pay, she decided. Her loins pulsed at the thought.

* * * * *

Allyson sat behind the desk, crude marker in hand, adding up columns of figures while Pitus stood over her shoulder, watching intently.

"According to this, you took in 322 *quitnums* last month—but you spent 353. Not good," she told the huge man.

He frowned when the U.T. translated her words. "Are you sure? Is this some slave trick?"

She shoved the paper at him. "See for yourself. Don't take my word for it."

He looked over the figures. From his expression, Ally could tell they didn't make a lot of sense to him. Like the 16th century people of Earth, most were illiterate, yet many could manage numbers in order to trade goods. Ally guessed that Pitus probably kept track of his business in his head and never wrote anything down because he couldn't.

Now he was being confronted by his lowly slave, and told that he was losing money. A Baktu's pride is second only to his greed and Pitus was facing that dilemma directly. If he got mad and punished this upstart slave as his instinct told him to do, he would continue to lose money.

His greed won out. "What would you do?"

"If it were me, I'd either raise my rates, or cut my expenses."

"What you mean, *expeenses*?" Apparently it didn't translate well.

"Well, look at this," she said, pointing. "You spent 88 *quitnums* on food for you and your staff. That's going to go up because you bought me. That's one-third your expenses. Do you really need four slaves to run this hotel? I spent most of the day sweeping—there was nothing else to do. Why not sell one or two slaves and cut down on slave ownership costs?" In her head, she was thinking, *I won't be around, so you'll save on my food bill.*

Pitus pursed his lips.

"You could raise your rates a little and charge your guests more for food and you'd have a lot more money," Ally went on, knowing that the more times she mentioned "money," the better off she was.

"You, uh, help me fix?"

Ally smiled. "Yes, as long as you treat me well. For example, no sex with the guests."

His eyes narrowed. He looked the naked woman up and down. Allyson could tell he was remembering her from her exposed position yesterday. After Beth left, he had moved his loincloth aside, exposing his rock-hard cock and rubbed it against her dripping pussy. Ally, still in the glow of her orgasm from Niktus, didn't struggle when he pressed the tip into her. She merely sighed and tried to adjust as best she could. When he plunged into her, she came again immediately with an even more powerful climax. For a huge man, his cock seemed just the right size.

Pitus stroked in and out rapidly until he came in a rush, braying like a mule. Ally felt his sperm gush out of her when he pulled back. His attitude changed then. He untied her and seemed to treat her with more deference.

Was I that good? she wondered. Regardless, she was able to use her sex—and her smarts—to show Pitus her value. Still, it was hard for the man to admit a woman—a mere slave—might have more talents than he did.

Ally waited, watching him decide, then held up the sheet, showing him his profits eroding away. Finally, he sighed and nodded. Another seven-foot tree, felled by a short, but smart and sexy woman.

"All right. But you no tell others. They get angry, get lazy."

Ally waited until his back was turned before she smiled and stuck out her tongue.

Chapter 27

Kate and her two companions rested by the trail. Sulala and Lilani weren't tired, but Kate was exhausted. She had been in decent shape when she left Earth, and assumed seven months asleep affected her more than she realized. Kate could also tell she was also about to get her period, dammit. It made her irritable. It also made her wonder. Do the women here get periods too? Are we that much alike?

She asked, tentatively, feeling a little ridiculous and was surprised to hear Sulala confirm that women here also bled regularly. They even had a name for PMS, *horanga*, which roughly translated into "slave's anger."

As they sat, Kate thought of ways she might ask them to help her understand how backwards people like the Baktu could overpower one to three people armed with phasers. She couldn't explain the weapons to the women; they wouldn't understand. Yet she knew the answer would be key to helping her rescue her crew instead of ending up just another prisoner.

"Besides their size, what makes men have such control over women?"

"They are very strong. We can't fight them." Sulala said.

"Don't they ever fight amongst themselves or with men from other tribes? How do they overcome them?"

"Oh, they expert at *paratan*," Lilani said.

"Pa-what? Paratan? What does that mean?"

"Hunting. Throwing rocks," Sulala put in.

"What? They hunt by throwing rocks?" Kate was dumbfounded.

"Yes, many are quite good. That is why they are better hunters than we are. We throw like girls."

"They throw rocks hard enough and accurate enough to knock down an animal?"

The native women nodded.

Jeez, no wonder Ally and the others had trouble. And I had to send her down alone!

"But we are learning," Sulala said. "That's how the hunting party you saw captured the *tomlatka*."

Kate remembered the small, furry animal that had looked like a raccoon. It wasn't much of a meal for the entire camp. "You don't use spears?"

"If we can," Sulala said. "But animals too fast. Rocks work best—if you can hit them in right spot—like in head."

"So the men can hit a small animal in the head while it is on the run?"

"Yes. I have learned some. I show you." The camp chief gathered up a few small rocks and stood. "That tree with the broken branch? See it?"

Kate nodded. The slender tree was about forty feet away. The trunk looked like a soda straw from this distance. Sulala whipped her arm in a sidearm motion. Kate watch the rock whiz past the tree, missing by a couple of inches.

"Ahh. I'm out of practice," she said. Her next rock thumped into the center of the trunk.

"May I try?" Kate had to see just how hard this was. She had skipped many a rock with her father at the pond behind their house in San Antonio. Taking a rock, Kate tried to use that same sidearm motion that she recalled from her youth. The rock missed the tree by three feet.

"Shit! That's hard." She tried again, adjusting her aim. The second shot missed on the other side, although by a closer margin.

"Not bad for first try," Sulala said. "Keep practicing. You will do better."

"The men are really good at this?" It was hard for her to believe.

"Yes. They have contests. There is one slave trader that travels through woods. He can hit a bird on a branch from fifteen *lumniks*. Many of my girls have been recaptured by this man and his partner. He hits them in head, foot—wherever he wants."

Suddenly, a light went on in Kate's head. "That's why you wear the helmet, uh, the hat. To stop them from hitting you in the head with a rock."

She nodded, reaching up to touch the hard bark shell. "Yes. I will not go back as slave. This might let me escape them. Not everyone likes to wear them."

"Too hot," Lilani complained. "I see men coming, I run. Get away."

"That's a good plan. I'll have to make one." Kate checked the sun. It was getting late. They had many more kilometers to cover before she would be in position across from the village they called Lakapit. She had to arrive there during the night to put her plan into action. "OK. I'm ready. Let's go."

* * * * *

Keltar called practice to a halt just before dusk. Jorja, soaked in sweat, felt like a wet rag. The heat made her bones too hot for her skin. "What I wouldn't give for a cold shower," she gasped.

"What shower?"

"Um, rain. A cold rain."

"Ahh. No rain here until *Makesa*. Two more *shatlaks* from now." The Ute still seemed to have some trouble with their measurements, she noted. "Come. We have way to wash up, like shower."

"Thank god." They left the other fighters and headed toward the dormitory. "What time is the fight tomorrow?"

"*Jamala*. When sun is high."

She guessed he meant noon. The hottest part of the day. If she had any chance to win, any at all, she'd have to do it quickly before the heat sapped her strength.

They went through a doorway, then walked down a corridor to a small room with a drain in the floor. A rope hung from the ceiling. "Take off clothes," Keltar said abruptly.

Jorja had just gotten used to wearing clothes again, but her need to clean up overpowered her sudden modesty. She stripped off the sodden garments and tossed them into a corner. She was surprised to see Keltar take off his loincloth and footskins as well. She couldn't help but stare at his large cock. She allowed herself a thin smile, remembering her efforts on board to make the computer generate the native hologram naked. *Now I've got the real thing and it's everything it's supposed to be.* Her libido reared its horny head for a moment. *Down, girl. He's not really a man. At least, I don't think so. But parts of him are a reasonable facsimile.*

Keltar picked up a bucket attached to the hanging rope and dipped it into a larger bucket of water in the corner of the room. He hauled on the rope and the bucket rose up toward a pulley. The bucket had holes on the bottom, allowing the water to dribble out. Keltar tied it off and waved Jorja under the water. She relished the crude shower. There was no soap, so she just rubbed the sweat off her body as best she could.

When the bucket emptied, he indicated she should return the favor. She filled the bucket and hauled it up, then admired the well-built man's efforts to rinse off the sweat and dust. Despite herself, she felt a heat in her loins, a familiar wetness that had nothing to do with the water dripping off her body. *You horny gal,* she told herself, *seven months in space and you're seriously thinking about fucking an alien.*

There were no towels. In this heat, they weren't really necessary. They padded naked back down the corridor, carrying their sweaty garments. Keltar appeared completely unabashed. He turned to the right and led Jorja to a door set in adobe. "Here my quarters," he said, opening the door.

It was a small room, about eight by ten. The only furniture it contained was a wooden chair, a box, and the bedding area taking up most of the back wall. Jorja turned to him. "Where am I supposed to sleep?"

"There," he said, pointing to the bedding.

"Then where will you sleep?"

He cocked his head. "There also. You afraid I sex you?" *Damn these ignorant Utes!*

"Um, no." *Then why am I acting indignant?* She felt the blood rush to her labia, causing more fluid to leak from her. *I'm afraid he won't,* she realized. She was sure he could smell her by now. His eyes locked onto hers for a moment before dropping down over her nakedness. She looked down as well and saw his cock swell slightly. A blush crept into her face and chest. She turned away.

"Come," he said abruptly, "we go eat." His cock drooped. He reached down into the box for another loincloth.

Jorja, grateful for the distraction, almost ran past him, then stopped short at the door. "Wait. I need clothes."

"Why? You woman."

"No, I'm a fighter. And fighters wear clothes."

He stared at her, then nodded slowly. He reached down and tossed her a loincloth as well. "What about my breasts?"

"Fighters don't wear loincloths on their breasts."

Great, she thought. Hoisted by my own petard of equality.

Chapter 28

Greta, her hands tied behind her, was practically dragged through the door to Gorshun's hut by the leash on her collar. "I'm coming, you bastard, I'm coming," she muttered as he hauled her inside. She had gone willingly, leaving a worried-looking Beth behind, but the slave trader seemed angry nevertheless. She had a bad feeling that he was still burning over Niktus' profit on the U.T.s and planned to take it out on her.

Can't we be friends? She knew she'd have to appeal to his masculinity to divert his anger.

Gorshun chained her to the wall near the bedding, then untied her hands. She rubbed her wrists and asked him, using the Ute, what was wrong.

"Niktus trick me, make me sell boxes cheap, now give me worthless slave in return," he barked.

"I am *not* worthless! I'm a mission...an important person in my own country."

"Look at your face. Damaged. And body—skinny, no hair. You look like girl."

"This is our custom where I come from. Body hair considered not attractive. And my cut on my forehead will heal up soon." *Not that you'll get to see it—we'll be long gone from here!*

"At least you have breasts! What about rest?" He groped with thick fingers between her legs.

"Wait! Slow down!" Greta remembered the vocal coupling between Beth and Niktus and knew that the species seemed quite compatible. Now she was about to find out for herself. She wasn't opposed to the idea, she just wanted him to be more gentle.

Gorshun wrapped a large arm around her back and held her close to him. The other didn't stop fumbling at her slit. "You my slave now. You obey."

The big man was too strong; she couldn't wiggle away. Her Earthbound tricks she used on so many men didn't work here. She couldn't be coy and tease this powerful alien. Greta tried to close her legs. He pulled his hand away long enough to slap her face. Her ears rang and her head ached. When his hand returned to her cunt, Greta didn't fight him. He pushed her down on her back, wedging his legs between hers, his fingers now beginning to draw some wetness from her, despite her discomfort.

"Please," she said, trying to push him away. "Go slower. I'm not ready."

He laughed. "What you ready for not important. I ready." Greta looked down and saw his erection growing—and growing.

"No, please, you're too big! You'll hurt me."

"You say you are woman. I find out." His fingers, rubbing against her clit, were beginning to have an effect on her, despite his crude advances. She began producing more fluid, coating his fingers even more, thus encouraging him.

He leaned down and kissed her erect nipples. Greta groaned despite herself. It felt good, even if he was an alien. He tickled her with his wet mouth, making her nipples ache.

Gorshun slid up between her legs, forcing them wider apart. The tip of his enormous cock touched her wet cunt.

She gasped and tried to pull away. His large hand held her by her shoulder, his weight pressed down on her body, flattening her against the bedding material.

As the bulbous head slipped past her nether lips, she sucked in air and tried to adjust to him. Greta had never had a man so well-endowed before. She had seen pictures on the Internet and wondered if they were real or digitally enhanced. Gorshun was not digitally enhanced. He was real and this was really happening.

I'm being raped by E.T.! Her mind screamed, even as he thrust in another half-inch. Greta found she couldn't close her mouth, as if by keeping it open she would be better able to accept him into her cunt. Thankfully, he was going slow, giving her time to adjust to his size. Though a tight fit, it didn't hurt yet. She just felt very full. She widened her legs a little more and altered her position slightly to accept him. She imagined her pussy was like the jaws of a snake, unhinging to swallow a gopher whole.

He pushed in a bit more. Greta could feel her fluid-producing glands working overtime to coat his enlarged member. Her mouth remained half-open, an empathic link to her cunt. He took his left hand off her shoulder and brought two of his thick fingers into her mouth. She sucked on them immediately. Now she was being fucked from both ends. Her mind was a confused jumble of want and need. Her conscious mind fled, endorphins kicked in.

His right hand came up to thumb her nipples and Greta nearly came right then. She looked down between her breasts to see he was still only about halfway into her. "Oh go', oh go'," she whispered around his wet fingers.

He pulled back for a moment and Greta felt a withering of her cunt, like a flower closing after the sun goes down. Her muscles gripped him, refusing to let him slip away and was rewarded when he eased himself forward again. Her channel enveloped him, welcomed him, invited him in for tea — anything, you can have anything, just don't leave yet.

He was beginning to pump now, just a fraction of an inch at first, up and back, up and back. With each tiny thrust, her cunt adjusted to him, made him slipperier. Her hips mimicked his actions. He took his fingers out of her mouth and kissed her. Greta kissed him back, hard. Somewhere along the way, she realized, he was no longer too big for her. His cock was stroking in and out now, each stroke carrying him farther into her. She wrapped her long, beautiful, hairless legs around him and hooked her ankles over his butt. Her hands wrapped around his neck.

"Fuck me, fuck me, fuck me," she repeated, lost now.

Gorshun grunted in response, his muscles contracting and expanding. His cock was thrust fully into her, then pulled almost all the way out. She hung on like she was riding a bull. He wasn't an alien any more in her mind, he was a man with a cock that fit her perfectly, a man who was bringing her to the edge of an orgasm that was coming at her with the power of worlds colliding.

Gorshun bellowed suddenly and thrust hard into her, spilling his seed. Greta's own orgasm was triggered a second later and they hung there, two lovers from different planets, finding a basic pleasure together. Greta's mind short-circuited for a few seconds with the power of it. The world was blotted out.

When she came to her senses, she could feel Gorshun's cock softening within her. Their fluids flowed out around it. He sank down into the bedding, resting his shoulder under her arm, being careful not to crush her with his weight.

"Oh my god," she breathed, her voice barely a whisper. "Oh my god."

"You good woman," he said. "I make fine bargain." Gorshun's mood had lightened considerably. All he needed to get over his anger was a small release of tension, she mused. With the puddle that Greta felt forming under her, she realized she'd better make that a big release of tension.

He got up and padded outside, probably to relieve himself, she thought. She felt spent and abandoned. "Don't men cuddle on this planet, either?" she said aloud. "Wam, bam, thank you, slave?"

Greta remembered her mission. She looked around the small hut. There weren't many places to hide a bag. The most obvious spot would be in the crude cupboards in the kitchen area, adjacent to the firepit.

When Gorshun returned, Greta volunteered to cook. He grunted and unlocked her chain. He sat, watching her as she went to the fire and stirred it, adding a few sticks of wood.

"What do you have to cook?" she asked.

"Nothing much. Maybe some bread. We must go to market, get food."

"I'll slice you some bread, then." Greta looked through the cabinet. The bread was on the top shelf, the animal skin bag on the bottom. Her heart beat faster. She made sure she didn't touch it. The bread was beginning to mold at the edges. Suddenly, she wasn't hungry. Finding a knife, she cut off the bad parts, then sliced him a hunk and brought it to him. He gulped it down eagerly.

Men get hungry after sex here as well, she mused. Now all they need is a football game on TV.

Her mind went back to the bag. She had to figure out a way to get their equipment out of the hut without being spotted. Being naked didn't help, either.

* * * * *

Kate and her two companions reached the spot she had identified on her scanner at dusk. Perfect. She turned to her new friends. "I have to go the rest of the way alone. It's too dangerous for you."

"It is dangerous for you as well. How will you avoid capture?" Sulala asked her, concern etched on her face.

"I, um, have some friends in the village who will help me," she lied, her face burning in shame. She couldn't share the details of her mission. They'd already violated the Prime Directive many times over. It was bad enough showing them the Ute, to whip out her phaser and give a demonstration would really freak them out.

Sulala, however, was no fool. She took one of Kate's hands. "I understand you can not say much. Your magic box shows that you come from a land that has many secrets we do not know about. Still, I worry that you will be captured by the slave traders no matter what you do. Will you let us go with you to protect you?"

"No, I can't. I would be worried about you and might fail to rescue my other friends. I hope you understand."

Sulala looked at Lilani, then back to Kate. Finally, she nodded. "Here," she said, taking off her helmet. "You take this. I can make another."

Kate was overjoyed. It might give her the margin she needed. "Are you sure?"

"Yes. Go with *Lamata*, god of woman."

"Thank you. I will never forget you." Sulala helped her put on the helmet and tied it under her chin. She hugged both women tightly, knowing she probably wouldn't see them again.

Then Kate turned and walked down the trail, leaving the two natives standing there, watching her. She went around a bend in the trail, then pulled her scanner from her backpack. It was three kilometers to the pod and two more to the village. She looked up into the sky and calculated. It was still too light. She walked further off the trail and sat down, her back to a tree. Holding her backpack between her legs, one hand on a phaser, she leaned back and closed her eyes.

"Soon, my crewmates, soon," she whispered and tried to get a little sleep. It was going to be a long night and she needed all her wits about her.

Chapter 29

Jorja woke in a tangle of bedding. Strange arms encircled her. She looked over her shoulder at the sleeping form of Keltar. Sometime during the night, he had crept up and spooned her. She smiled, flattered that the man found her attractive. On Earth, it was hard for a six-foot-tall, 180-pound woman to get a date. Men seemed afraid of her Amazonian proportions. Being a black belt didn't help, either.

Here, she was just another petite woman, dwarfed by most of the men on the planet. She felt almost kittenish, an emotion she hadn't experienced since before she hit sixth grade and found she towered over most of the boys.

She tried to disentangle herself from Keltar, but only succeeded in arousing him. He pulled her closer and mumbled in his sleep. His erection rubbed against her leg. What is it about men and morning hard-ons, she wondered. She was foolish to sleep in the nude, she knew. But the damn loincloth was so restricting, she had to ditch it. They had started out well apart on the bedding. Keltar really was the perfect gentleman. He said it was because she belonged to another owner, but Jorja could read the signals he was sending out. He wanted her, more so because she was a fighter, like him, she surmised. Her strength turned him on. But he maintained a careful distance.

Sometime during the night that distance had evaporated. Jorja tried to unwrap his arms without waking him. Instead, he merely tightened his grip. Now his hard cock poked between her thighs. He snored softly in her hair. She didn't dare move. One of his hands opened and cupped her breast, a thumb brushing her hard nipple. Her body betrayed her. She was becoming aroused at the gentle hands of this giant.

In his sleep, Keltar began thrusting his hips in minute arcs, following some crude dream. His cock touched her hot slit and Jorja sucked in her breath. "Keltar," she whispered. "Keltar, wake up."

She should be shouting, she knew. Pounding on his arms. But there was something incredibly erotic about the entire experience. She wanted to wake him and yet she wanted to feel him press against her just a little while longer. Unconsciously, she eased her legs apart, letting the tip of his cock slide over her wet cleft, causing her labial lips to engorge with blood. Back and forth he stroked in tiny movements. Jorja bit her lip. Her clitoris came to attention. She eased her right hand down to touch it. It was as hard and smooth as a small, round river pebble. She reached down a little further, opening her fingers and felt the tip of his cock as it thrust forward. In seconds, her fingers were soaked in her own juices.

Gee, she thought, if I just tipped my hips back slightly and helped guide him, he would slide right in. *No, I'd better not.* Even as she denied her feelings, her body betrayed her again. His hand pulled away from her breast slightly and she found herself leaning forward to follow it. Naturally, that changed the angle of her hips and his cock began to nip inside her a fraction of an inch, the head easily parting her wet lips.

"Oh my," she breathed. "You're going to get into trouble with my boss." She giggled behind her free hand, the other remaining between her legs, touching the mushroom head of his hard cock as it appeared and disappeared into her.

He began thrusting harder now and Jorja suspected that Keltar had awakened and was only pretending to be asleep in order to avoid any moral conflicts over his desire for the Earthling. She let him fuck her, his cock sliding in further and further until he was tight against her ass. His slippery member was a perfect fit.

His left hand came around to her mound to hold her in position as he continued to thrust, all the way out, then back in again. Jorja rubbed her clit, relishing the waves of pleasure that washed through her. *God knows I've needed this! I've been in space too long!*

Keltar began making noises in his throat, which drove Jorja toward her own climax. There was something about being fucked from behind by this powerful man that sent her swooning. He rolled her over, bringing her to her knees, her head pressed down against the pillows. This allowed him to thrust deeper within her. She could feel his cock sliding all the way in and out again, causing a vibration in her clit that built quickly.

Her orgasm struck her an instant before Keltar stiffened and his cock erupted deep within her. "Jesus, god in heaven!" she shouted, jerking as if electrocuted. He held her tight for a minute, then eased out of her. Fluids rushed out and soaked the bedding.

He spoke to her in that strange language. As Jorja fumbled for the Ute, she realized she understood a few words. "Sorry... Gulnark... angry... asleep." He was trying to apologize for giving her the best sex she had had in years.

"*Dabala, nektu vas,*" she responded without thinking, knowing it meant: "Don't worry, it's all right."

She thumbed the switch on the U.T. "You've learned some of our words," Keltar was saying. "That's good."

"Yes, I seem to be picking up some basic terms," she said, getting up. "Excuse me, I have to pee." She padded outside naked, unconcerned that other fighters might see her. It was freeing somehow, being naked all the time in a world where nakedness was the norm. She squatted over the latrine, which was really nothing more than a hole carved into the ground, and released her bladder.

Jorja was beginning to like this culture, despite its drawbacks. She didn't like the way women were treated, of course, but not all men were cruel bastards like Gulnark. If more men were like Keltar, there could be some meaningful reforms made. She could help the downtrodden women, just as she helped the natives of Ghana build a safe water supply when she had been with the Peace Corps so many years ago.

Careful, girl, that violates the Prime Directive!

Damn! Her conscience was right. Too bad. She would love to help these people. She wondered what would happen when the full complement of Earth scientists arrived. Wouldn't they violate the directive just by being here? How could they not help shape the culture when they came in with their binoculars, listening devices, strange dress and manner? And isn't that the same thing that Jorja and the away team had been planning to do before they were so quickly captured? So why is it so wrong to try to help people?

Too many questions! Jorja shook her head as she padded back to Keltar's room. These issues should be left to the experts. My job is figure out a way to get back to the pod and fly out of here. She must not forget that.

When she came in, Keltar was talking in low tones to a stranger she hadn't seen before. She sat on the bedding and pretended not to listen. Instead, she eavesdropped, hoping to learn something that could help them escape. Without her U.T. handy, she couldn't make out much. But she did hear the words for "bet" and "profit."

The stranger left. Keltar approached her, bringing the Ute with him. "Good news, Fighter Jor-ja. The odds favor you to lose."

Jorja wasn't sure how that was good news.

"Many people were impressed with your fighting skills, but many also believe Gulnark is a weakling," he continued. "They do not believe you could prevail against a trained fighter. This makes our plan clear. Already, our agents are out placing bets on you to win. I will pair you with a good fighter, but one who is not too tall. If you can defeat him, we win many *quitnums*."

"But what about my efforts to buy our freedom?"

"Freedom? No. You must have owner."

"We just want to get away. Can't you help us?"

Keltar shrugged. "We put up money. What do you have to trade?"

Jorja rocked back on her heels. She hadn't expected this. "If I win you a lot of money, I figure that's what I have to trade."

He shook his head. "Not enough for all of you. That takes much profit. Perhaps we could win enough to buy one of your friends."

Jorja stared at him as she fought back tears. One of her friends? *Now what? Will I have to fight and win three times to buy them all?*

Chapter 30

Beth and Niktus strolled through the market, looking over the selections. She had no idea what would taste good, as the fruits and vegetables of this planet were unusual, to say the least. One vegetable looked like spoiled eggplant, but Niktus assured her it was delicious when cooked and mixed with nuts.

She carried a pouch over her shoulder and her "master" would buy items and place them in her bag. He carried nothing, she couldn't help but notice. In fact, all the men with their slaves walked free, letting their women carry everything. Like the other women, Beth was leashed to her owner, although he carried it loosely. Did these men think that if women weren't leashed, they would suddenly bolt? Or maybe it was just a sign of control.

A paleness caught her eye and she looked up to see Greta, naked and leashed as well, following Gorshun into the market area. "Master," she said. "May I say a greeting to my friend?"

He glanced up and spotted Gorshun. "No, I think not. Gorshun is still angry with me."

He pulled her away. As she looked back, she saw Greta staring at her and patting her market pouch. *Does that mean what I think it does?* The leash tightened, and Beth stumbled to catch up with Niktus.

Beth watched as a slave was instructed to bend over a cart and accept the hard erection of her master. Where just two days ago a scene like that had shocked her, now it seemed commonplace. She wasn't sure if she would ever feel comfortable having sex in public, but she imagined she could eventually get used to it.

She paused to watch the scene, telling herself she was just being an anthropologist. Of course, seeing the hard cock glistening as it thrust back and forth, hearing the squishy noises of their coupling aroused her as well. The woman's satisfied expression told Beth that she was not at all embarrassed by the public display. She caught Niktus' eye and flushed red as he smirked at her. They moved on.

Shortly before the sun hit its apex, the crowd began to migrate from the market over to the main square. Greta and Beth were led to the low platform, although their owners stayed well away from each other.

Beth saw the tall, gaunt hotel owner arrive. She was disappointed not to see Ally with him. Instead, he had a native woman following behind him, leashed and placid.

Posts had been set up in the center of the platform, tied with ropes to make a crude ring. The *jamalut* was about to start.

The crowd milled around patiently, swelling in numbers until it seemed as if the entire village had arrived. Suddenly a hush fell over the crowd, then whispering began. Beth looked over to see a small crowd approaching. She recognized Jorja immediately. Right away, she could see their engineer wasn't naked. She wore a loincloth and another wrap around her breasts. The crowd seemed to be amazed by this behavior. They pointed and tsked.

Beth felt proud of her crewmember. "You go, girl," she whispered, then louder as she approached, "Hail to the Earth woman!" She raised a fist above her head. The men near her glared. Niktus yanked her chain, silencing her. Jorja saw her and smiled.

A man got up onto the platform and began speaking. Beth fished her U.T. out of her bag and began listening.

"Baktus! Today we have two special contests for you! Our champions Klasdor and Ripatus will fight to decide best of the best. Both men are in top shape and ready for this event. Much profit can be made if you bet correctly!

"Before that event, however, we have a novelty match for you. You have seen the strange women from faraway land called Earth. They look different, have many strange customs. They say women are not slaves in Earth! Shocking! One of them even dared to fight her owner! Many said she should be punished—tied to post and beaten until she learns to obey." The crowd cheered lustily.

"Others say let us see how she does in ring with real fighter! Much profit possible! So today, we present Slave Jor-ja—queen of Earth!"

Jorja, fighting her overwhelming nervousness, clasped her hands over her head and danced, "Rocky"-style, as if her show of bravado would increase her confidence. She climbed up onto the platform and stepped between the ropes into the ring. Keltar came over and caught the announcer's attention. He leaned down and listened while the trainer spoke into his ear. He nodded and straightened up.

"As you know, Gulnark has allowed this contest, rather than punish his slave himself. To make sure the fight is fair, he's decided to let Keltar chose her opponent from among the well-trained and professional fighting corps." Some in the crowd cheered, while others were not fooled and jeered Gulnark for not fighting her himself.

Beth looked around and saw Dolnark and his son near the platform. Gulnark looked embarrassed.

"Jor-ja's opponent has been carefully chosen. She will be fighting against one of Keltar's top young fighters, a man who has won his last three fights! *Tangut!*"

A man separated himself from the small group and clambered up on the platform. Beth blanched. The man looked tough and strong. Fortunately, Tangut did not tower over the engineer. She guessed his height was about six-three. Still, he appeared to be a formidable opponent.

"Now, as you know, these strangers have been in our village only a few days. There was not time for Jor-ja to learn our fighting style. Besides, she has one of her own, from Earth, that she calls '*kar-at-tee*'. Therefore, we declare this fight to be 'no rules'." The crowd cheered again.

"The contestants will battle until one of them is unable to continue. Men, place your bets now! The fight will begin in nine *lunnits!*"

The crowd went wild. Money was waved, men talked excitedly with each other, making wagers and backing them up with *quitnums*. Men whom Beth assumed were bookies collected money and wrote down bets on parchment.

It took ten minutes for all the activity to settle down. Finally, the announcer held up his hands. "Men! Are you ready?" The crowd yelled back. "All right!" He turned to the fighters, eyeing each other in the ring. "Jor-ja, are you ready?" She nodded, never taking her eyes off Tangut. "Tangut?" He nodded.

"All right. Fighters, begin!"

Tangut charged at Jorja, remembering how much trouble the Earth fighter had had with the much-taller

Maknar during practice yesterday. Jorja just slipped away from him, kicking him in the stomach as he went by. Tangut shrugged it off and came in again. Again, Jorja danced away, this time rapping him in the face with a backhanded fist.

Tangut angrily shook his head, then came in more cautiously, trying to punch or grab the smaller woman. She dodged his first blow, then kicked him hard between the legs. The breath whooshed out of him and he staggered away. Jorja was on him in a flash, kicking through his knee from behind, forcing one leg down. She spun and tried to kick him in the head, but Tangut remembered seeing that trick and ducked. Her kick sailed overhead, spinning her off balance.

As she struggled to right herself, he charged, knocking her to the mat. He jumped on her, but she wasn't there. She had rolled away at the last second and now had scrambled to her feet. He started to get up, only to be met with a kick to the head. He scuttled back out of reach.

The crowd gasped. Tangut reached up and found he was bleeding from the nose. Enraged and embarrassed, he lost control and charged the woman, arms outstretched. Jorja planted her left foot and brought up her right into a hard front kick, aimed directly at his stomach. It was like running into the end of a log. The breath was forced out of him and his head dipped. Jorja grabbed him behind the head and brought it down to her knee, rising up from the floor, the same technique she had shown Gulnark. The collision could be heard all over the hushed square, the thwack of knee against bone. Tangut, unconscious on his feet, slid to the mat in a heap, his head bouncing once.

There was a collective gasp from the crowd. No one seemed to be able to believe it. A mere slave woman had defeated a man! A trained fighter! Gulnark looked pleased with himself, as if to say, "See? That's how she defeated me!"

Klasdor, standing with the other fighters, suddenly jumped up onto the platform, his face a mask of rage. "I fight you!" He declared. He raised himself to his full seven-foot height over the gasping Jorja. Keltar scrambled up and entered the ring. "No! You must fight Ripatus!"

"I fight them both. Her first! She dares to fight like men! I show her!" He approached the woman, brushing aside Keltar as if he wasn't there. The crowd roared their approval. Jorja cowered back into a corner. There was no way she could defeat this man. He must weigh 325 pounds!

Klasdor stalked toward the woman. Everyone seemed to be at a loss as to what to do except the crowd, who continued to cheer lustily.

Suddenly, a huge explosion rent the air. Heads turned as one as a portion of the street leading to the square simply dissolved into smoke and dust. Some men near the blast site held their hands over their ears, mouths agape. The dust continued to swirl in the hot air. Everyone in the crowd stared, not comprehending what was happening.

Beth, Jorja and Greta stared as well, not quite believing it themselves.

Out of the dust and smoke, a lone figure came striding toward the crowd, skirting the bomb crater. As it approached, Jorja, from her better vantage point, was the first to recognize the strange apparition.

"Captain!"

Beth and Greta took up the shout. "Captain! Captain Dyson!" All of the crew women were stunned that Dyson would disobey orders to come down and try to rescue them.

Now the crowd could see that the figure was a woman, dressed like the *Bakchari*, the free women of the forest. On her head was a helmet of bark. She continued to approach and a man near her bent down to pick up a rock. Without pausing, Kate aimed and fired the phaser in her hand. There was a bright light and the man staggered and fell down. The crowd drew back. In the hush that followed, Kate held up her U.T., the volume turned up loud and announced.

"Don't fuck with me. I have PMS and a gun."

Chapter 31

The men, true to form, quickly overcame their initial shock. They began looking at each other and nodding. A few moved into position, ready to surround the approaching woman. Several picked up rocks, too many to shoot.

Kate, never breaking stride, held up her scanner and pressed a button. Another huge roar went up, heads swiveled toward the sound. The blast came from just outside the village. Prevailing winds carried some of the dust and smoke toward the crowd.

"Stay back or I'll blow you to hell," she said, waving the scanner, to make sure they knew who was responsible for the explosions, which she hoped were completely out of the range of their experience. Kate was bluffing, of course. She could never kill any of these people. She had two more hidden C4 charges, both outside the village. All she had to do was make them fear her for just a few more minutes and she just might be able to get her team away from here.

"Release the Earth women!" she shouted. She fired off another hidden charge, this time on the other side of the village. With each blast, however, the effect on the aggressive men seemed to diminish.

Niktus glanced uneasily at Beth, then looked across the crowd and caught Gorshun's eye. Niktus could tell from his expression he wasn't about to release his new slave. Gorshun yanked hard on Greta's leash, to warn her she'd better not move.

The men continued to surround Kate. One tall man to her right slipped a rock into his hand and flung it before she could spot him. The rock bounced off her helmet. She turned and fired, stunning him to the ground. A humanoid directly in front of her sidearmed a rock while she was distracted and struck her forearm. She gasped and nearly dropped her phaser. She shot him as well.

Kate was becoming desperate. The men were not cowering at all. Now she understood how Ally had been taken so easily. Despite her modern weapons, she was outnumbered. She might be able to hold them off for a little while, but soon a rock would hit her face or her hand and she'd be helpless.

She whirled and fired at the first sign of movement, dropping men who approached or tried to stone her. By now, the first men she had stunned were slowly getting up, letting the others know that the blinding white blasts weren't fatal. Kate glanced down and checked her phaser. It was half depleted already. If they didn't back off and let the crew go soon —

Suddenly, another phaser blast split the crowd. Gorshun screamed and pitched forward. Greta stood there, phaser in hand, swinging around in an arc as the crowd fell back. She ran to the edge of the platform and tossed an object up to Jorja.

Jorja recognized it as a phaser immediately and caught it in mid-air. Klasdor, standing with his mouth open, snapped it closed and charged her. Jorja didn't have time to reprogram the phaser, so she dropped down and spun, extending a leg out. Klasdor tripped over it and fell headlong into the ropes. Jorja jumped up, slapped her finger over the grip scanner and punched in the code while the angry fighter struggled to his feet. He turned and bellowed as he thundered at her again. The engineer dialed in a "3," raised the gun and fired and near-point-blank range. There was a blinding flash of light as the fighters collided. Jorja bounced off as the huge body of Klasdor crumpled to the ground.

The crowd gasped. These women seemed to be sorcerers! Pitus, taking in the events with horror on his face, turned and ran toward his hotel.

Jorja signaled to Beth, who turned and grabbed Niktus' arm. "Please, master. Don't get hurt. Let me go." He opened his hand as if the leash was a deadly serpent and Beth ran toward Kate.

The men surrounding the captain fell back when the second, then the third mysterious weapon appeared in the Earth women's hands. The women formed a circle, their backs to each other, forcing the men back even more.

"Where's Egerton?" Kate shouted.

"Come on!" Beth led the way toward the hotel. The crowd parted, uncertain now as to what to do. Many glanced over to see the unconscious form of Klasdor in the ring and decided the wisest course would be to let them go.

The astronauts rounded a corner in time to see Pitus run up the steps into the hotel. "Come on! We've got to hurry!" Beth shouted, not knowing what Pitus might do to Ally.

The burst through the door and stopped dead. Pitus held Allyson in front of him, a crude knife pressed against her throat.

"Drop your lightning sticks or I'll kill her," he said.

"Do as he says! You guys just go without me!" Ally implored.

Three phasers were raised higher to point at his head, which towered above the frightened woman. Beth held up her hand. "Wait. Let me talk to him."

She approached slowly. "Look, Pitus. All we want to do is get out of here and go home. We don't want to hurt you. It wasn't supposed to end up like this."

Pitus shook his head. "I need her," he blurted out. "Niktus was right. She knows numbers. Without her, I can not make profit."

"Sure you can. She's told you what you need to do. Just follow her advice," Beth said soothingly, aware of the hair-trigger tempers behind her. "Besides, you don't want it getting around that you listen to a slave, do you?"

Uncertainty crossed his face. He shook his head imperceptibly. His pride would not allow that.

Kate heard noises and turned to see the crowd approaching. "We have to go, doc," she said urgently. "Company's coming."

"Let her go, Pitus. You don't want to kill her. Then you'd never make a profit."

"I paid good money for her!"

Jorja spoke up. "Tell Keltar that with my profits from the fight, he should buy your slave first. He and I have agreement. You will make profit."

He hesitated. "This is true?" She nodded.

"All right." Jorja suspected that he just wanted a way out. Pitus dropped the knife and stepped back. Ally ran out from his arms and hugged Beth. "Thank god!" She turned to Pitus. "I'm sorry. I didn't want it to end this way."

"Come on! Let's go!"

The women, together again for the first time since their ill-fated mission began, had no time to celebrate. They ran out the front door as the crowd neared, then turned and sprinted down the street toward the edge of the village. Greta, still limping, slowed them down. The men followed, keeping a respectful distance.

"Dammit! They were supposed to be too scared to follow us," Kate gasped as they ran. She didn't say any more, but everyone knew what she meant. The bobsled would hold just three of them. With the men close on their heels, it would be nearly impossible for the last two women to hold them off long enough to make it to the first pod in order to blow it up.

"Hang on, I've got one charge left," she shouted. Kate spotted the marker as they ran past the edge of the village. She looked back, gauging how close the crowd was, then thumbed the button. The blast, directly in front of them, was smaller this time, but it had the desired effect on the humanoids—for a few seconds, anyway. They paused, confused, and appeared to talk it over for a moment. Then they regrouped and came on.

"Don't they ever get scared?" Greta gasped. She had doubts that she'd be able to run all the way to the pod.

They could see the pod in the distance now, across the flat plain. Only about two clicks away, Kate thought, her mind racing to figure out how they were going to pull this off.

"Listen!" She shouted over the sounds of their feet thumping the ground, their breaths rasping in their throats. "I'm going to stay behind with Ally! We'll take all the phasers. You guys jump in and take off. We'll met you at the site of the other pod."

Beth had expected the captain to say something like this. "No, captain. You can't stay. You have no rapport with these people. You wouldn't last five minutes."

"She's right," Jorja put in. "Beth and I have the best chance." She looked over at the doctor and as if on a silent signal, they stopped running.

The others slowed and turned. "Come on! They're gaining on us!" Greta shouted, even as the gap between them widened.

"No, we'll stay and give you time to get away," Jorja said. "Here. Take my phaser. I wouldn't want to violate the Prime Directive." She tossed it to Ally.

Kate wanted to order them to keep running, but she knew they were right.

"All right. We'll come back for you. Run in another direction, try to make the trees."

"No," Beth said. "I'm a doctor and an anthropologist. I'm going to stay until the next ship arrives, in about a year."

"Me too," Jorja said. "They respect me as a fighter. Together Beth and I can learn a lot from these people."

There was no time to argue. "All right," Kate said, knowing this was a very brave and selfless act. Tears came to her eyes. "But I'm putting you both on report." Jorja and Beth grinned. Then the captain and the others turned and ran off.

Chapter 32

Beth and Jorja stood facing the approaching crowd. The doctor was glad to see Niktus among the pursuers. Jorja recognized Keltar. In seconds, they were surrounded.

"Don't chase them, they will kill you with their lightning sticks!" Beth shouted. "We will stay with you."

"I will fight any man here," Jorja declared, shouting out the first thing that came to her mind. "Unless you are afraid of a slave woman?"

A man lunged at her, she side-stepped and used his momentum to throw him to the ground. Keltar ran up and kicked the fallen man. "How dare you attack my fighter? This woman belongs to me! She has no right to fight without my permission!"

The distraction worked. The men stood, breathing hard and looking confused. Some stared at the three retreating woman with great interest.

"You can't let them get away!" A man at the edge of the crowd shouted. A handful of humanoids took off after the trio.

Another man, facing Niktus, waved a finger in his face. "These slaves need to be punished!"

"I will take care of my slave, as I am sure Keltar will deal with his fighter," he said coldly. "I would not tell you how to treat your slaves."

The crowd broke up. Most followed Niktus and Keltar back to the village with the Earth captives, while about a third loped after the other women.

Ahead, Kate was happy to see the tactic worked. She looked back and counted a dozen or so men running after them. "Set your phasers on heavy stun," she said. "Let's not fuck around with these bastards any more. Ally, you pilot. Greta, you stand with me to hold them off."

Greta started to object. As commander of the away team, she should be allowed to remain pilot. Wisely, she kept her mouth shut, remembering the accident that caused all the problems.

When they reached the bobsled, Ally yanked open the canopy and pulled out the bulky space suits covering the rear seats. These would have to stay behind. There would be no time to don the constricting garments. She jumped into the pilot's seat and started takeoff procedures.

Kate and Greta faced the advancing crowd. As soon as they were in range, they fired. Two, then four men fell. The rest scattered. Some picked up rocks, but the range made it difficult for them to get a throw off before they were zapped. In seconds, the crowd was routed.

"Come on! We're ready to go!" Ally shouted.

The officers jumped into the rear seats and strapped themselves in. The humanoids who were still standing began to drift closer, only to shy back when the big engine fired. Kate reached up and slammed the canopy shut just as the bobsled started its run. With flaps on maximum, the craft soon lifted off and rocketed into the sky.

"Yahoo!" Greta shouted. "I was never so glad to leave a place!" Her exuberance shut down immediately, as the realization hit her that they had left their friends behind. "Can we go back for them, captain?"

Kate shook her head. "No. Beth was right. We must think of the overall mission. If we tried to go back, we'd probably get ourselves in trouble again. No, we must go home. NASA is sending another ship out for them."

No one said anything for a while after that. There was really nothing to say.

The pod raced up through the atmosphere. In minutes, the deep black of space filled the canopy. Kate shivered as the cold cut through the thin metal skin. "Too bad we didn't have time to put on our spacesuits," she murmured. She was worried about what they had left behind. Besides the suits and the pod, they'd left Beth's medical kit, the Utes and a couple of radios. Strange devices to the natives. She hoped it wouldn't cause the humanoids to turn on Beth and Jorja, accuse them of black magic.

Soon, the comforting shape of the *Letanya* came into view. They docked and waited for the air to return to the docking chamber. When the canopy rose, it was a somber group of astronauts that climbed out.

They walked single file down the corridor to their cabins, where they donned clothes. Allyson and Greta felt strange having coveralls on again, but neither spoke of it. Within a few minutes, they were all on the bridge. Without thinking, Kate flicked on the main screen, letting the transponders overlay the camera image of the village. Two yellow dots were moving down one of the streets leading to the square, surrounded by dozens of humanoids. They watched in silence for a few minutes.

"I'll tell you one thing, captain," Ally finally said. "The next ship that NASA builds is going to have pods big enough for all the crewmen at once."

Heads nodded. They were so close to getting them all out!

Kate checked the board and found two messages waiting. Sighing, she called them up in order. "Care to watch your captain get fired?"

Hunter's mottled face appeared on the large screen. "Houston, calling *Letanya*. I've given you a direct order, Captain Dyson. I want you to return with the ship immediately. Under no circumstances are you to use an escape pod in that risky manner. We're sending another ship to your location with a complement of Marines and it can reach them within six to eight months. I want you to acknowledge this message as soon as you get it. I don't think I need remind you of the effect this kind of insubordination could have on your career. This is Houston, over and out."

Silence settled again over the trio. Kate checked the logs. As she had anticipated, that message had been received just ten minutes after she had jettisoned away in the pod. The second message had been received a full day later.

"Well, we've got one more. No doubt this will be my official dismissal." She brought up the other message onscreen.

The smiling face of John Phillips filled the screen. Kate's brow furrowed. She had expected Hunter again.

"*U.S.S. Letanya*, this is Houston. I hope you get this message, captain. It's important. When word got out about Admiral Hunter's orders to you to abandon your crewmates and head for home, the reaction was swift and overwhelming. The general consensus was, 'American astronauts do not leave their buddies behind.' The country rose up with one voice and backed your decision to go down to the planet, despite the risks. The president removed Hunter from his post just four hours ago and has put me in charge of the mission until you return."

Kate had trouble believing what she was hearing. She heard a soft "All riiiight!" from Ally as they strained to hear the rest.

"We all hope and pray that you succeeded. We're sending another two ships to you now. The *U.S.S. Saratoga* will arrive in six months, the *Sovereign* a month later. The *Saratoga* contains a boatload of Marines just itching to free your crew women. Scientists are aboard the *Sovereign*, ready to study the planet and it's people. If you hear this message, please respond if you can. The entire country is waiting to hear from you. This is Houston, over and out."

A ragged cheer went up from Ally and Greta. Kate was simply too emotionally drained to react. She took a few minutes to compose herself, then gave her crew women a thin smile. "Well, I think we'd better check in. I only wish we could've rescued them all."

Kate asked Ally and Greta to stand behind her as she dialed up the radio-telescope. "Houston, this is *Letanya*. Three of us are back aboard ship. As you can see, Commander Egerton and Mission Commander Hanson are safe. Hanson did suffer some injuries, but they are not considered serious. It was a risky operation, I admit. We were successful in getting all five crew members away from the village, but unfortunately, we had to leave Dr. Reyes and Lt. Commander Smith behind. They have been taken back into the village by the humanoids."

She paused, blinking back tears. "With the personnel and equipment we have, I'm not sure another rescue attempt will be successful. These humanoids are aggressive and strong and aren't intimidated by our display of modern technology. I'm willing to try, but after our close call, I'm afraid if we go back, we could be recaptured. Please advise us as to what course of action you recommend. This is *Letanya*, over and out."

She turned to the others. "You can send personal messages while we wait. If you prefer, you can record them in your quarters." They both nodded and left the bridge. Kate sat alone, wondering what ordeals the astronauts were going through down on the surface. Were they being beaten? Raped? Maybe even executed?

Kate put her head in her hands and cried.

Chapter 33

NASA agreed with the captain. Don't risk another rescue attempt, she was told. "You are ordered to come home, *Letanya*," Phillips said gently. "Everyone here knows that you'd like to stay in orbit. But you know that you'd have to go into cryosleep anyway to conserve air and food, so you wouldn't be any help to Dr. Reyes or Lt. Commander Smith. And after you woke up long enough to watch the *Saratoga* rescue your friends, you'd face another seven months of sleep to get home. Cryosleep isn't recommended for such long periods. There really isn't any more you can do for your friends. Please come home. Houston, over and out."

Kate bit her lip. NASA was right, there was nothing they could do here. "OK, you heard 'em. Looks like we're going home."

"Is that really right?" Greta asked. "We've only been out here eight days. Seven months in cryosleep and we go home a full six weeks short of our mission parameters? Can't we explore some other worlds while we're out here?"

The captain sighed. Greta, always the go-getter. No doubt she could just write off the two lost crew members and go on. Kate couldn't and she doubted Allyson could either. "No, we have our orders. And we're short-handed. Besides, we owe it to our grateful nation. I'm sure they'd like to congratulate us on our rescue efforts." The sarcasm oozed from her. A tear tracked down her cheek. Angrily, she wiped it away. "Frankly, I don't like it either, commander. I don't want to leave them down there, and I don't want to hang around up here, helpless. It's time to go home. Leave the rescue to the Marines."

They left orbit four hours later and aimed the ship for home. When they were clear of the solar system, Kate pushed the ship into warp and watched as the stars blurred. "Time to take a nap, girls," she said, and led them down to the sleeping chamber.

They all undressed silently, their thoughts heavy. Kate helped the others in, then locked down the capsules. In minutes, they were in a deep sleep. Kate took one last look around. "I'm sorry, Beth, Jorja. I'm so sorry," she whispered to the silent room. Then she crawled into the cocoon and locked down the hatch.

Chapter 34

Jorja and Beth marched back with the crowd toward the village. They heard the roar of the bobsled behind them as it took off.

"Do you think we're in for it?" Beth asked nervously.

"Maybe," the engineer responded. "Maybe we can bluff our way out of this." Jorja was dismayed to see the figure of Gulnark approaching.

Gulnark, with his father right behind, marched right up to Jorja. "You *baramus!*" He shouted, his face contorted with hate. "You dare you harm my people, and run from me? I'll show you who is master!" He backhanded her across her face. Jorja just had time to bring up her hand to partially block him, but didn't counter, though she had an opening to give him a knee to the groin. She bent with the blow, her eyes tearing up.

Beth shrunk back as other men surrounded her. Some had telltale burns on their chests from phaser blasts. She could see they clearly wanted to punish her on the spot.

"Kill them!" a man shouted, trying to incite the others. "They will destroy us!"

"They aren't our kind!" said another. "They have magic—bad magic!"

Gulnark, emboldened when Jorja didn't fight back, tried to slap her hard across the face. Someone grabbed his arm.

"Gulnark, if you want to fight her, talk to me." Jorja turned to see the square face of Keltar.

"She belongs to me!" Gulnark screamed. "You can't interfere!"

"Very well," he responded, letting go of his arm. "But first, let's settle our bets."

Two bookies appeared silently on either side of Keltar. Gulnark blanched.

"You owe me 200 *quitnums*," said one.

"And me 100," said the other.

The scene caused the men around Beth to stop what they were doing long enough for Niktus to push through the circle. "I will take charge of my slave now," he said calmly, keeping his eyes steady on the irate men. They knew she belonged to him, so they edged back just slightly, though they didn't stop glowering. Fortunately, the confrontation between Gulnark and Keltar distracted them.

"I-I do not have the money on me at the moment," Gulnark stuttered. He looked at his father, who just shrugged.

"How much did you pay for your slave?" Keltar asked.

"Two-fifty," Dolnark said.

"I will pay your debts in exchange for the slave Jor-ja," Keltar said calmly.

Gulnark again looked to his father for approval, then nodded quietly to Keltar.

And just like that, the confrontation was over. The crowd walked into the village, Keltar holding Jorja's arm possessively, and Niktus leading Beth by her leash.

Beth's heart leaped with her gratitude for her "master." He stared down those thugs and exerted control over the situation. She didn't mind being led. On Earth, it would be degrading; on Devon, it gave her a sense of belonging, of value, that the other villagers respected.

Jorja, of course, felt the same way toward Keltar. And now he owned her! Her loins ached with the thought of what lay ahead for them tonight.

Tonight, apparently, was too long to wait for Keltar. No sooner had they reached the village then he pushed her up against a wall and indicated she should bend over and brace herself against it. Jorja reddened, and glanced at Beth, who graciously turned her head away and followed Niktus down the street.

Jorja remembered the last time a man had tried to force her to have public sex. She kicked the shit out of him. She wasn't about to do that to her rescuer, yet she wanted to let him know that she considered herself a fighter, not a slave.

"Fighters don't have sex in public," she declared, her gaze steady.

Keltar stopped as if slapped. Several in the crowd gasped at the effrontery. As one, they turned to see Keltar's reaction to such talk. "Then we fight," he said after a few seconds.

This was the last thing she expected to hear from the taciturn trainer. Yet how could she have accepted anything else? She had challenged his manhood, his honor, in front of the town—now she had to fight the man she was falling in love with.

"When?" She asked, her voice betraying her emotion.

"Now. The main fight scheduled today has still not occurred and I think the crowd would enjoy another exhibition bout. Let's go."

The crowd roared their approval. Jorja found herself propelled along toward the main square once again.

"I don't want to fight you," she whispered, hoping no one else could hear.

"You left me no choice," he said out of the side of his mouth.

"But one or both of us might get hurt. You might damage your new fighter," she responded urgently. He said nothing, just continued to haul her along beside him. Jorja could see his jaw twitching.

They reached the square. She was dragged up onto the platform and thrust into the ring. The crowd filled in quickly as news of the fight spread. To the side, Jorja could see Klasdor and Ripatus watching, their arms folded over their massive chests. They talked in low tones to each other, as if making a bet on the outcome. She scanned the crowd and saw others betting, holding up fingers and nodding.

Jorja spotted Beth and Niktus entering the square. She was glad to see her—before the bout was over, she might need a doctor, she mused.

She squared off with Keltar, her heart pounding. She didn't want to do this. She wanted to make love to him, not fight him. Yet, she couldn't bring herself to be treated publicly like a mere slave. She had worked too hard to set herself apart from the native women of this planet—Beth too, for that matter. She felt she would be fighting for the doctor's honor as well.

It seemed to be a no-win situation. If she fought hard and lost, Keltar probably would hurt her badly. If she won, Keltar would never forgive her for making him lose face. She could see the determination in his face.

Suddenly, Jorja understood what she had to do.

Chapter 35

The umpire shouted for them to begin and Jorja and Keltar came together quickly. Keltar made a grab that Jorja easily parried. She had an opening for a kick to the stomach, but she let the opportunity pass. Instead, she tried a sweeping hook kick, a flashy, but often ineffectual move. Keltar blocked it easily, then pushed her off-balance. She fell to the platform and quickly rolled away before he could fall on her.

He let her rise without interference. He came again with a technique Jorja had seen him do many times in practice — a high-low combination that often fooled the rookies. She blocked the feint to her face, then tightened her stomach against the blow that followed. Jorja pretended it hurt her worse than it did. She staggered back as the crowd cheered.

Keltar allowed himself to become cocky, and followed up quickly with a grab that was designed to push her into the ropes. She spun around and kicked, holding back as she did, feeling her foot connect with his midsection. Startled, he let go of her and backed away, shaking his head.

He grinned at her, as if he knew what she was doing. She felt they were on the same wavelength. For some reason, Jorja found this to be highly stimulating. She couldn't believe it. They were in the middle of a fight, even if she was just making a show of it, and the interplay was making her hot. Maybe it's because she was doing it for Keltar and he knew it. She was letting him save face and that really was the only possible solution to this dilemma he created when he tried to exert his command over her.

I'd have sex with you anytime, just not in public – we Earth women haven't come that far yet!

He came in again with a technique he had taught her just yesterday—a sweeping action that knocked most opponents off their feet. Jorja had taught him a counter to it—a quick jump up, legs tucked tight, a fraction of a second before his leg struck the back of hers, causing him to fall off balance. When she landed a second later, she had been in a perfect position to counter-punch him. This time, she let his technique work and landed on her back, slapping her right arm down to absorb the blow.

Jorja pretended to be hurt. She rolled around on the platform, while Keltar strutted about, waiting for her to rise. The umpire finally stepped in and declared the trainer the winner.

He graciously helped her to her feet and they left as the crowd roared its approval. Jorja "limped" along with Keltar's arm about her waist. His touch electrified her. They walked to the training compound alone, as Klasdor and Ripatus made their way into the ring for the big fight, drawing the crowd's attention.

"Don't you want to see them fight?" she asked.

"No. Klasdor's going to win. The bets are down already."

"The fight's fixed?"

"No. But Klasdor is a very good fighter. I trained them both. I know who will prevail. I'm more worried about you."

"I'll be OK. I'm not really hurt, you know."

"I know. I wanted to thank you for not challenging me there. I would have lost my position as trainer if I had lost to a woman."

"I figured as much. I really didn't want to fight. you" She straightened up after they were inside, out of sight. Jorja put a hand on his strong broad face. "I'd enjoy having sex with you — but we just don't do it in public where I'm from."

He nodded. "You are quite different from Baktu women. I must remember."

They went into the shower room and cleaned up. They left, naked and dripping wet, letting their hands roam over each other's bodies. Jorja was dripping wet in another part of her anatomy as well, she noticed. Their playfulness caused Keltar's erection to grow. It was like a club sticking out from between his legs. Jorja was fascinated by it, like a snake charmer might be.

They practically fell into Keltar's room, stumbling to the bedding. The water had evaporated already from their skin. They clung together as they rolled as one, Jorja kissing the trainer, feeling a true kinship with this humanoid like she had never felt with an Earth man. Here was a big strong man she could hang onto.

He fondled her breasts, causing an electric current to spark between her nipples and her cunt. She had to have him, now.

She wrapped her legs around him, opening her cunt to his hard cock. He teased her for a few minutes, letting just the tip slide past her engorged labial lips as her cunt sucked at him.

"Oh, please," she begged. "Put it in, put it in."

"Perhaps this would be a good time to discuss men's superiority to women," he said, humor in his voice.

"Oh, please, not now! Just fuck me!"

His cock slipped out and back a half-inch, driving her to distraction. "Now, after your miserable performance in the ring, would you not say men are the better fighters?" he teased. "And women should stay at home and care for the house, cook for their masters?"

Jorja could hardly concentrate on his words, her entire being so caught up with the feel of his cock. "You bastard," she gasped, grinning.

"Calling your new master names? Looks like I'll have to punish you." With that, he thrust his cock hard into her. She gasped once as it filled her completely, then her breath left her as she exploded into a powerful orgasm. More stars surrounded her head.

Keltar still wasn't finished. He kept stroking his huge cock into her, bringing her to another climax in a few seconds. Then another. Finally, when she couldn't imagine coming again, she felt him erupt into her, causing yet another orgasm to rip through her body.

"Oh, Jesus! I can't stand it!" she cried out, hugging him tightly to her.

They clung together, finally able to express their love for each other. Jorja felt her small sacrifice in the ring was well worth it.

Chapter 36

Six months and three days later, the *U.S.S. Saratoga* eased into orbit over Devon. Four times the size of the Letanya, this, by all accounts, was a battle ship. It bristled with armaments, including lasers, space cannon and heat-seeking rocket-torpedoes designed to work in airless space. The lasers could cut through a planet's atmosphere and destroy structures — or people — on the ground. The *Saratoga* normally carried a crew of 25, but the addition of the Marines brought the total up to 40.

Unlike the *Letanya*, this ship had two large shuttles, capable of carrying ten men in each. Both shuttles would be used in this mission. Nine soldierswould fly down in the first shuttle, followed closely by the second, carrying six soldiers. The remaining space on board was reserved for the hostages, as they had come to call the former crew women of the *Letanya*.

"Listen up, soldiers," barked Sgt. Dale Baker once the Marines had shaken off the effects of cryosleep and gathered in their staging area in the shuttle bay. The beefy black sergeant spoke with the authority that fifteen years in the Marines had given him. "You've had your beauty sleep, now it's time to earn your pay. The lieutenant will be in shortly to give us a final briefing, but I just want to remind you: You know you've all been hand-picked for this mission. I expect you to honor the code and use your heads. I don't want anybody to get hurt out there."

Lt. Carl Nystrom opened the cargo access doors and strode in. Immediately, the group jerked to attention. "At ease," he said as he walked up the steps to the platform to stand next to the sergeant. "Everything OK?" he asked. Baker nodded.

"All right, listen up." He eyed the fifteen Marines, dressed in full battle gear, their heavy-duty phase rifles nestled in their arms. "This isn't going to be a bug hunt or a weenie roast. We're dealing with intelligent beings, not unlike ourselves, only these guys are big and aggressive. We don't want to be the Ugly Americans, but we're not going to be pushed around, either. We're going to go into the village where we picked up the transponder signals and ask politely for our astronauts back. Only if they refuse will we get medieval on their asses."

The Marines cheered upon hearing that. They didn't come all this way to pussyfoot around with the natives, regardless of what the mission parameters were.

"You all have pictures of Dr. Reyes and Lt. Commander Smith, but my advice is, look for the only good-looking women on the planet—from what I hear, these native gals are hairy as apes." There was derisive laughter all around. "The *Letanya* reports both Reyes and Smith have Utes, so presumably we'll be able to communicate with the people, who call themselves the *Baktu*. That's what I'll be doing—talking. You soldiers are to back me up. That's it. I don't want anyone to be quick on the trigger. All weapons will be set on stun. And no one fires his weapon unless I fire first, understand?"

There was reluctant nodding all around. A couple of them winked at their buddies and one showed his fingers were crossed.

Nystrom looked at his watch. "All right. We're dropping down to a lower orbit and should be ready to go in about ten or fifteen minutes. If anyone has to take a leak, now's the time." He strode off the platform.

"All right, you heard the man, maggots! Let's check those weapons. All must be kept in the safe position until you hear from me or the lieutenant. We don't want to start an intergalactic war with these guys."

The men—and a few women—milled around trying to hide their pre-raid jitters. Corporal John Sisco caught the eye of his friend, PFC Joe Henderson, and they eased away from the group.

"You think we'll see any action?" Henderson asked his buddy.

Sisco shrugged. "Maybe. Depends on the humanoids. They're supposed to be big mother-fuckers. They could tear your arm off."

"Is it true they keep women as slaves? On leashes?" Henderson's eyes gave away his overactive imagination.

"Yep. That's what I hear. Pretty cool, huh?" They guffawed together.

"Hell, instead of fighting 'em, I may join 'em."

Across the room, quite a different conversation was taking place between Private Jane Emerson and her friend, PFC Luisa Rodriquez, two of the three female Marines aboard.

"I'd like to get one of slave-owning bastards in my sights," Emerson was saying, "I'd blast him to hell."

"Yeah, but I hear those big fuckers have cocks the size of firehoses. Be a shame to waste that."

"Maybe we can find one for you to fuck before we shoot him." They both laughed.

Soon, the ship was in position. The shuttle bays opened. The Marines stowed their weapons and strapped themselves into the jump seats. Sisco would pilot the first craft, Corporal Ben Asmor, the second.

"Listen up," Nystrom said once the soldiers in the first shuttle had settled in. "We're going to be landing just outside the village for maximum shock value. When we come to a stop, we want to come out strong and tight and secure a perimeter. Just like textbook, OK?"

"Yes, sir!" The men—and three women—shouted in unison.

"We're not going to fuck this up, are we?"

"No, sir!"

"All right. Let's go hunting for some lost lesbos!"

The shuttles were launched one after another into the silent vacuum of space. They turned and dipped down toward the planet below. The soldiers couldn't see where they were going in the windowless aft section, so they just waited, staring at the walls or grinning at each other to show how brave they were.

Soon, the telltale buffeting began. Sisco adjusted his trim and rode it out as if he had done this a thousand times before. After several bumpy minutes, the craft broke through into blue sky and glided down. Sisco and Asmor extended the wings, increasing the glide coefficient. The ships fell uneventfully until they hit 25,000 feet, then encountered more turbulence. A soldier turned green and vomited quietly into a barf bag. Others hooted at him. In minutes, the turbulence ended and the crafts straightened out.

"Eight thousand, prepare for landing." Sisco barked into the intercom. There wasn't much the soldiers needed to do except hang on to their shoulder straps.

The twin crafts swooped in to picture-perfect landings, nearly side-by-side on the dusty plain less than a kilometer from the village. A donkey, strapped to a cart holding two men, brayed and reared up. The men jumped down from the cart and watched as the donkey fled in fear, dragging the cart behind it. They appeared stunned as the crafts slid to a stop not two hundred yards away.

As soon as the dust settled, the doors opened and strange men jumped out and surrounded the crafts. The humanoids knew they were outnumbered and outgunned and ran for their lives out into the plain, away from the village.

The soldiers watched them go but did nothing. Weapons tracked their movements across the plain.

"All right! Remember, I want all weapons on heavy stun only. You got that?" Everyone nodded reluctantly. "Jones, Emory, stay with the ships and monitor the radio! The rest of you maggots, follow me!" Baker barked.

Led by Lt. Nystrom, the remaining twelve men and women jogged east, toward the village. The heat baked down on the group. Loaded down with equipment, they were soon gasping, despite their extensive training in preparation for the mission. Six months in cyrosleep can take a lot out of a person.

When they reached the edge of the village, Nystrom stopped them and began deploying the soldiers with hand signals. The streets here were strangely deserted. Up ahead, the soldiers spotted some natives running away from them down the dusty avenues. The group split up according to strict deployment protocol—three peeled off and began to run around the village so they could approach from the south. Two more went left and two went right, to cover their flanks.

"Stay frosty, people. They're inside watching us, you can be sure of that." He punched the button on the radio. "Emory! You read me?"

"Roger, sir. Loud and clear."

"We're going in. Keep your eyes open."

"Roger."

They entered the village, guns up. Soldiers ran from dwelling to dwelling, watching for any movement. They had been told these natives had no sophisticated weapons, but they were taking no chances.

They approached the main square. There were a few dozen men and women there, milling around. Beyond them, Nystrom could see the three soldiers driving other natives from the south side of town into the square. The men wore animal skins as loincloths. They stood proudly, defiantly watching the soldiers. The Marines could see the narrow ridge on their foreheads and the flattened ears. Otherwise, they looked quite human. The women, cowering behind them, were all naked.

One of the soldiers whistled.

"Remember your orders," Nystrom said evenly and pulled out his U.T. Fastening it around his neck, he strode toward the crowd.

"We come from Earth," he said.

A man detached himself from the group. He was tall, nearly seven feet, and broad-shouldered. He easily towered over the six-foot-tall lieutenant. Nystrom held his ground, though he wanted to step back. He guessed this man weighed more than 300 pounds.

"Why are you here?" The humanoid said.

"We come for the Earth women," Nystrom responded.

"They wish to stay," the giant said.

"We'll be the judge of that. Where are they?"

There was a sudden movement in the crowd. A figure was coming forward. All weapons immediately swiveled in that direction. Nystrom was the first to see that it was a woman. Short and dark, she was dressed in animal skins around her waist and breasts, and a thin leather collar around her neck. The lieutenant could also tell she was very pregnant.

She approached the soldiers, stopping to say a few words in that melodious language of the planet to the giant. Nystrom's Ute registered it as, "I'll take it from here, *Klasdor.*"

Nystrom frowned. The picture he had memorized flashed into his mind. "Lower your weapons, soldiers," he ordered. Confused, the men complied.

"Dr. Reyes, I presume?"

The woman nodded. "Lieutenant. I'm surprised to get such a extensive rescue party," Beth replied.

"Are you all right?"

"Yes, although I have a little back ache now and again." She rubbed her swollen belly.

He shook his head slowly. "So it appears the species are quite compatible with ours."

"Yes, I'd say so."

"Where's Lt. Commander Smith?"

"She's at the training facility."

"Training facility?"

"Didn't your briefing include her training in karate? She's a big hit here, as you might imagine. She's teaching the men how to fight, Earth-style."

Nystrom again shook his head, as if to clear it. "Well, if you could lead us to her, we'll collect you two and be on our way."

"Um, no, lieutenant. I want to stay. I think you'll find Jorja does too."

Nystrom was taken aback. "We've come more than two million light years at considerable expense and effort to rescue you—and you say you don't want to go? I really don't think you have a choice."

"I think we do." She patted her stomach again. "As you can see, I'm not in any condition for cryosleep. The baby won't wait. It will be another two months before I have it. Once it's born, I'm not about to take it away from its father." She turned and signaled to a middle-aged man, who separated from the crowd. "This is Niktus, my, er, husband." She almost said "master," but caught herself in time. She didn't think the soldier would understand.

"Earthling," Niktus said in heavily accented English, nodding down at the smaller man. "The Baktu welcome you."

Nystrom was speechless. He expected to be greeted by two very grateful women, being rescued from a horrible ordeal. Instead, he finds they're happy with their situation. Before he could react, a movement caught his eye. The group swiveled to the right, weapons came up again. "Easy, Marines," he said.

"Ahh. Here comes Jorja now," Beth told him.

The tall figure coming toward them wore a loincloth, but her breasts were bare. Nystrom heard another whistle from the soldiers. She was drenched in sweat and had a cloth tied around her short brown hair. Smooth muscles rippled along her arms. She strode right up to the lieutenant. He tried very hard not to stare at her breasts.

"Our rescue party?" she inquired—but not in English. Nystrom's Ute gave the translation.

"Yes," Beth told her in the same language. "They say we'll want to go home now."

"We are home," Jorja said.

"Speak English, please!" Nystrom snapped. "You're Americans! Probably the most famous Americans in the space program. The papers call you, 'the Abandoned Astronauts.' Everyone is anxious to see you home safely."

"Thank the American people for me," Jorja said in English. "But I am home. I've got it made here. You could say I'm a VIP. So's Beth. She's the town healer, you know."

"You can't possibly want to stay in this backward environment!"

"It's not so backward. Just different. We've come to like it very much."

"But, but—what about the Prime Directive?" Nystrom sputtered.

"Except for Beth's medical skills, we're not using anything from Earth anymore. We don't need the Utes, so we buried them, along with the radios that were left behind. We burned the pod. We're living just as the natives do."

"I thought women were treated quite badly here, that no American woman could stand it."

"At first blush, that appears to be true," Beth admitted. "But women have far more power than you would think. It depends on the woman, I guess — and their mast — I mean, man. In our cases, we're highly regarded, so we get extra perks. We're using that power to help all the women."

Beth decided not to tell him about how she was still led around by her leash when in public, often naked like the others. He wouldn't understand. It wasn't humiliating, it was a belonging, a sense of acceptance, of being loved. And she did love Niktus. He was a kind and gentle man, despite his fierce appearance.

She thought of the women in the forest, whom she had been helping to return to their villages without punishment. Kate had radioed her from orbit to tell her about them. Beth and Jorja had used their influence to convince elders to educate cruel masters in proper slave-owning etiquette. In the last six months, slaves have been given more avenues to see problems resolved. They were making progress, but they weren't done. Beth wanted to stay and see it through. Did this violate the Prime Directive? Possibly. She preferred to think of it as gently steering the people toward a more humane way of life.

"Um, we're going to have to report in on this one," Nystrom said. He looked around. The men were still staring at Jorja's breasts. The female soldiers seemed to be eyeing the loincloths of the nearest natives. Nystrom's face grew hot, but he kept his mouth shut.

"Why don't you all stay for dinner? We could introduce you to what I like to call roast beast."

Nystrom nodded dully and excused himself. He stepped back a few paces and pulled out his radio.

"*U.S.S. Saratoga*, this is Red Leader. Come in."

"This is *Saratoga*. Captain Richardson here."

"Uh, yeah, captain. Tell Houston we have a problem. The astronauts have gone native on us."

Chapter 37

Kathryn Dyson stepped down from the ramp, trying not to cry in the bright autumn sunlight of Earth. Her legs were still a little wobbly, made more so by the thousands of cheering fans who had turned out to greet the returning women. She spotted Brian and a very tall Donnie, who both ran up to hug her.

"Oh, you can't imagine how much I missed you two!" she gushed, her heart overwhelmed with emotion. "And Donnie — look how big you've gotten."

"Welcome home, Mom, but please, call me Don now." He had matured so much in the last two years, she realized.

"Let's get you away from here. I have big plans for you," Brian said. She blushed and smiled, tears in her eyes. He kissed her, right there in front of millions, and squeezed her ass briefly. Kate didn't even mind.

Allyson and Greta stepped out behind her, bringing another cheer from the crowd. They stood and basked in the attention before being whisked off for some much-needed private time with their families.

This was not the welcome they had envisioned. Kate had expected to be vilified for leaving Beth and Jorja behind. Instead, it was NASA and its design of the pods that took the heat. The fact that Kate went down alone, against orders, and nearly succeeded in rounding up all her crew fit in perfectly with the American image — tough, bold, unafraid, and willing to do anything to help her crew members.

The true story would not have come out if America had relied just on Kate's report. She gave a minimal summary of the rescue. Allyson sent Kate from the bridge to rest from her ordeal with a wink and called up Houston and gave them the complete version of events. America decided Kate was a hero. If it hadn't been for an overcrowded pod, the mission would have been a rousing success.

No one blamed Kate when she arrived home. NASA quickly ordered that all pods be made larger—which meant the scout ships would have to be larger as well. Another advancement for the space program.

Despite the attention, Kate didn't feel like a hero. She still felt guilty for leaving Beth and Jorja behind. She went through the interviews with the media and appeared on talk shows to benefit the program, but her mind and spirit weren't in it.

It wasn't until the reports came back from the *Saratoga* that Kate learned the truth. By all accounts, the two women they had left behind were happy on Devon.

Her fear that they would be punished proved to be groundless. Although the Baktu culture was based on male superiority, the Earth women were considered to be valuable property. Would you damage a Van Gogh or a Stradivarius?

Once Beth had the medical kit, she was able to partner with Niktus to aid many of the villagers. She felt she was making a difference and having the support of Niktus made it much easier. When she learned she was pregnant, rather than being dismayed at the thought of having an alien child, she was overjoyed that she could share her love with the older man.

Jorja had several more fights, mostly exhibitions and warm-up spots on the cards. She was treated with as much respect as any man, especially after an incident in a village bar when a drunk man claimed the fights were fixed and tried to show that a man who wasn't in on the scheme could defeat her easily. After Jorja threw him into a table, twice, her legend only grew.

They realized that the image of this race that they first observed was really a sham. Men were in charge, but behind the scenes, women wielded considerable power. Like Ally did with Pitus, women who had some worthwhile talents used them to support their "masters." In exchange, the men would give them great latitude in the house, out of sight of the other men in the village.

The sight of women being led around by leashes was simply a tradition, a holdover from earlier, darker days. Women actually enjoyed this display because it showed how much she was valued by her master.

Epilogue

Many years later, recently promoted Captain Allyson Egerton returned with a newer, faster ship to Devon to visit her former crewmates.

She touched down near the village, which had grown considerably since her first visit. A welcoming procession arrived. By now, the villagers were used to visitors from their "sister planet," Earth. When Beth and Jorja saw it was Allyson who had returned, they were overjoyed.

Beth introduced Jamel, her son, now six, and Berda, her daughter, three. Jorja had a son, Kendor, age two, and was pregnant with another child.

Both women were naked and both wore their collars proudly. Allyson felt a little embarrassed to be overdressed in her NASA coveralls. She stripped down to tee-shirt and shorts in the heat and they strolled back into the village for a feast.

"You are both looking very pleased with yourselves," Allyson remarked. "You've really adjusted well to this culture."

"Yes, we had to travel two million miles to find men we could love," Beth admitted. "I'm not sure why. I think it was because men on Earth are so hung up on body image. Just because I was carrying a few extra pounds, some men acted like I didn't exist. Before I joined NASA and started traveling the heavens, I probably had ten dates. None ever went anywhere."

"I had the same problem for different reasons," Jorja told Ally. "I'm a big-boned, bold, beautiful woman. I think I intimidated men. At six feet, there aren't that many men who were willing to be seen with me. And when they learned I could kick their butts if I had to, that only made it worse. Earth men are so insecure."

Ally laughed. "And to think we were worried when we had to leave you behind. I can't tell you how that tore us all up."

Beth nibbled on the inside of her lip. "Yeah, I was worried too, at first. But deep down, I think I wanted to be left behind. I felt there was so much more I hadn't accomplished here yet."

"My reason was more practical," Jorja said. "I knew I had to stay behind because I was the best equipped to survive here. What started out as a sacrifice led to a very satisfying life."

"Do you think you'll ever go home?"

"No, except for a visit," Beth said. "And I'm not sure I can handle being away for so long."

"The new ships can make the trip in two months. Some don't even bother with cyrosleep," Ally told her.

"I'd be interested in returning, but not to stay. Like Beth, my life is here. I finally feel like a normal-sized woman on Devon. I wouldn't want to go back and deal with all those problems again."

"I'm impressed. And frankly, having you two as our goodwill ambassadors is doing wonders for our relationship with the Devon planet. Thanks to you, the elders have even agreed to let us build a starbase here."

"We may be seeing a lot more of you, huh, Captain?" Beth said. "You may be stopping by to partake in our local delicacies. Maybe even try out one of our well-endowed men?"

Allyson blushed. "Hush, now. I hope a starship doctor isn't advocating interstellar sex!

"Oh, hell no, Captain," she laughed, patting Jorja's ample belly. "After all, we wouldn't want to violate the Prime Directive!"

About the Author:

J.W. McKenna is a former journalist who took up penning erotic romance stories after years of trying to ignore an overly dramatic—and often overheated—imagination. Married and living in the Midwest, J.W. insists with a grin that polite people would be shocked if they knew what kind of writing was being done in their town.

Printed in the United States
24642LVS00002B/67-711